WAITING
IN DEEP

Sandi Morgan Denkers

PublishAmerica
Baltimore

Softcover 9781630049393
PUBLISHED BY PUBLISHAMERICA, LLLP
www.publishamerica.com
Baltimore

Printed in the United States of America

For my parents with love

Nancy Hughes Morgan
July 5, 1944-July 10, 1970

Buford Morgan
March 6, 1944-September 4, 2000
Writer and Poet

and for

Wanda & Danny

*Though he was God's Son, he learned trusting-obedience
by what he suffered, just as we do.*

*Hebrews 5:8
The Message*

*Hope you enjoy
Waiting in Deep* ♡

[signature]

A special thank you to Mary Denkers, my mother-in-law, who read, proofed, and added valuable insight. Thank you: Trula Gahagan for your friendship and prayers; Dalene Parker and Joyce Cowley, for your input and for contributing in many ways to the manuscript's readability; Tonda Bailey and Karen McGill, your enjoyment of the manuscript (extremely rough at the time) kept me going long after you returned the awkward binder. Wyonnia McKissick, thank you for sharing your soulful heritage with me through years of friendship and fellowship. You didn't know I was taking notes, did you? Thank you, Tim, Rachel, Stephen, Elliott and Stephanie, for listening to me talk about my book year after year.

Thank you to those who encouraged me along the way either by reading rough draft portions or asking how the book was coming along: Tom Payne, Dalton Ford, Kay Clair, Patty Hammett, Jan Dehippolytis, Melodie Fulbright, Kimberly Dillard, Cindy Sneed, Florence Steen, Tyler Kirby, Diana Flegal, Ruth Kimbrell, Earnette Gyde, Renee Long, Kerry Holliday, Janice Smith, Larry Denkers, Joy Davis, Renee Willard, Brenda Morrison, Debbie Garrett, and Wanda and Rick Garcia.

Of course, endless gratitude to Jesus who stayed with me in Deep, then brought me out.

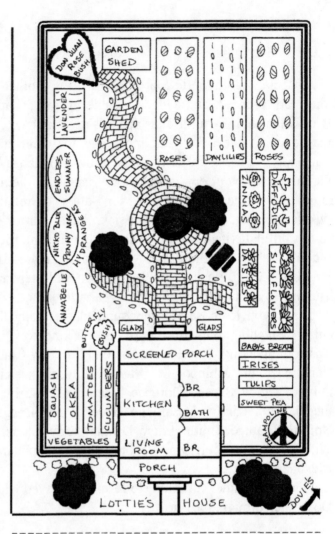

LOTTIE'S HOUSE

MT. BRAYDEN, SOUTH CAROLINA

This is my story.

Death tried to kill it;
Grief tried to drown it;
Pride tried to erase it;
Pain tried to forget it;
but
Deep saved it.

My story grew words while waiting in Deep
And now my words have wings to fly.

Lottie Johnson,
Age 96

Mt. Brayden Times
Sunday, August 15, 1943

Three Year Old Among Victims

An afternoon car accident on Salter's Creek Road has left three people dead. Circumstances surrounding the crash have left investigators asking for help. Saturday, August 14, Jerome Williams and his 3-year-old daughter, Wyonnia were walking on Salter's Creek Road to visit a relative. According to investigators, approximately 3:30, 74-year-old William Draper was traveling north on Salter's Creek Road when he apparently braked and over-corrected, sending his car crashing into Williams and his daughter.

Draper was transported to Mt. Brayden General Hospital where he later succumbed to his injuries. Both Jerome Williams and his daughter were pronounced dead at the scene.

If you have any information regarding this fatal accident, please notify the Mt. Brayden Police Department.

Azalea

Chapter One

1972

While Flower Power swept the West Coast, petals of velvet germinated with little notice in the deep, rich south. The soil's aroma traveled underneath Lottie's wide-brimmed straw hat, hovered, then dissolved like an invisible gift. She straightened her tight back. Clouded sweat drops rolled down the deep crease between her eyes while bees hummed and birds chattered and the winds of change breezed in.

Rebecca let the screen door slam.

"Hey, gal. How was your day?" Lottie pulled a thin handkerchief from her apron pocket and wiped her face.

"It was okay. Can I help you before we do our homework?" Rebecca asked.

"Depends on how much we got. Homework is more important than flowers."

"We only have spelling and math."

"Good. Let me finish with these jonquils and we'll cut back the roses. Then we can do the homework." She leaned in closer to Rebecca. "Mrs. Brown ain't suspicious, is she?"

"No, ma'am. She don't even ask me no more if I want two sets of homework. She just hands them to me."

"That's good because I don't want people meddling. Only a few people know I supply your mama's shop with flowers and that I'm teaching you about gardening." She patted Rebecca's silky blonde hair. "It's for the best."

"Why?"

"Because when you live in a small town, it's hard to keep people out of your business. Seems like news sprouts legs and travels door-to-door like an eager salesman. Once it reaches Is That You? Styling Salon, you can kiss your secret goodbye; it spreads like syrup on a mound of lopsided pancakes."

Rebecca giggled. "That's called gossip."

"Yeah, and Dovie next door, is the queen."

"What about Leander and Odelia?"

"They just as bad. Who told you about them?"

"You did."

"Well, keep that to yourself." Lottie dabbed her forehead. "Sometimes I have to sneak around out here so Dovie don't see me and start filling me in on the latest news."

"At least you can run back inside and get away from her."

"No, I can't. Five minutes later she calls me on the phone. I got no escape."

Rebecca put her hand on Lottie's shoulder. "You need to tell her gossip is ungodly, like you told me."

"I did. I said those exact words to her yesterday. She said, 'It just so happens I've been elected to serve as an usher at church and because of that, I've been stricken with conviction.' I had to cover the phone, I laughed so hard. She said, 'Last night I was on my knees, even with this arthritis.' I said, 'Dovie, God ain't looking at your knees, he's looking at your heart.'"

"Preach it, sister."

"I said, 'I hope you ain't playing around with God because he don't play.'" Lottie got up off her knees and stood. "I knew she done got a attitude because when she does her mouth don't never stop. She said, 'I ain't playin! Hattie's sewing my outfit right now. They didn't have one my size and that did cause me some embarrassment, but I made up my mind and said, no, I ain't gonna let my size stop me from doing God's work. Come Sunday, I'll have on my white skirt and blouse and little matching hat. When we pass the plate, I'm gonna be humble, hold my head high, and walk ever so softly.'"

Rebecca laughed and sat down beside the pile of clippings. She thought for a minute. "How can you be humble and hold your head high?"

"You can't. I told her when it's offering time she needs to take the center aisle because it's a tight squeeze by the windows."

"Miss Lottie! I hope you didn't hurt her feelings. Guess what? Mama pulled one of my teeth last night and I pulled the other one out myself. See?" She stretched open her small mouth and bent her head back.

"I see that."

"Now we look like twins."

"At least you can grow yours back. Don't be like me. Keep your teeth brushed or you'll be sorry."

Lottie gathered her work gloves and clippers then walked to the bench. She sat under the shade of the pink dogwood and rested her eyes. The warm breeze jostled new, tender leaves. When she opened her eyes, Rebecca stood by the rose bush.

"Will you tell me the story again?"

"For you, I'd tell it a hundred times." She dried the back of her neck and dabbed her throat. "My husband, Jerome, bought me that climbin' rose bush the year we got married."

"That was 1939." Rebecca walked to the bench and sat down.

"Yes, it was. He bought it for me because he liked the name. We thought it was called Don Jewon, until your grandma told us it was pronounced Don Won. Me and Jerome laughed about it some, but then he got quiet. He only had a little learning like me. Well, anyway, that climbing rose bush has been growing now for all these years and it still produces the deepest red roses you can find. Every time I look at that beautiful bush, I think of Jerome. I can see his handsome face and his full, soft lips. I wish you could have seen him."

"Was he tall like you?"

"Oh, he was much taller than me." Lottie pulled her straw hat farther down on her forehead. She cleared her throat. "Yes, sir. He was a fine man."

"I'm sorry I made you sad."

"Honey, you didn't make me sad. You help me remember things. Things I don't ever want to forget." She looked into Rebecca's large brown eyes. "We didn't get a thing done out here, but I don't care. Push the wheelbarrow over there and we'll have a glass of lemonade before we do our homework."

"Yes, ma'am." Rebecca pushed the rusty wheelbarrow past the hydrangeas and under the lean-to.

Lottie stepped onto the back porch, tossed her dirt-clad gloves in the drawer of the porcelain-top table, then washed her hands in the large green bowl on top of the washstand. She looked at the bulging wringer washing machine as she dried her hands on a dish towel. Her eyes scanned the colorful display of Bell jars, milk-white vases, cobalt blue jars, and clear glass bowls. "Let's clean up this messy porch tomorrow. I had a hard time getting my clothes rack out from beside the washer this morning, and my work table looks like a shelf in the Salvation Army Thrift Store."

"Okay, I'll help." Rebecca followed her into the kitchen. "Can I have some cookies, too?"

"After you wash your hands."

Rebecca lingered at the sink until Lottie set the glasses of lemonade on the table. She dried her hands, stood in front of Lottie, and held them out, palms up. The back of her cool, damp fingers rested in Lottie's hands. Sometimes she had to wash them again, but today they were clean.

"Have a seat. Only two cookies. And remember to go brush your teeth when you're finished. Promise me you'll always take care of them because your smile is a reflection of all that's inside you."

Rebecca licked the lemonade from her upper lip. "I promise."

Soon books were opened, papers cluttered, and eraser shavings scattered. Lottie listened to Rebecca explain long division again and watched her work out several problems on the paper between them. Then Lottie worked out her own problem and did it correctly.

Rebecca looked surprised. "How do you catch on so quick?"

"After you leave I do more problems and then I write the spelling words twenty-five more times."

"No wonder you're so smart."

"Well, thank you. You're the first person who's ever called me smart." Lottie laughed. "What's after math?"

"Ten new spelling words. They're hard, too."

"Maybe you should write them twenty-five times extra like I do."

Rebecca smiled. "They're not that hard."

An hour passed between them until, at last, the work was finished.

Rebecca played "What a Friend We Have in Jesus" on the piano while Lottie enjoyed the sound of chimes: high, low, soft, and pleasant. Her head rested on the back of the comfortable couch. She closed her eyes and remembered herself with her back straight, hands positioned, and her right foot stretched as Mama sat close by and smiled approvingly—

Rebecca stopped playing and swirled around on the piano stool. "I'll get it," she said as she sauntered across the room.

Lottie heard a man's voice. "Who is it?"

"It's Edgar!"

"What?"

"It's Edgar!" Rebecca said louder.

"I heard you." Lottie stood, exhaled, and trudged toward the door. "Party's over," she muttered.

Edgar recognized the dark-eyed girl who stared back at him but he couldn't remember her name.

"You're Miss Lottie's cousin," she said through the screen door.

"That's right. What's your name again?"

"Rebecca."

"Well, come on in, Edgar," Lottie said. "You don't have to stand outside."

He stepped through the doorway and set his small suitcase on the floor. His mouth was dry. The pockets of his pants hid cold, clammy hands that fidgeted with change and soft lint balls. "So, how you been, Lottie?"

"Fine. How about you?"

"Pretty good. Working here and there."

"You got a place to stay?" Rebecca asked.

Lottie's eyes fixed on her. "You planning on taking him home with you?"

Rebecca's face reddened. "This must not be any of my business. I think I'll go home." She turned and walked to the kitchen. A moment later, she had her notebook and books stacked in her arms. She leaned close to Lottie. "I love you. See you tomorrow."

"Love you, too."

"Bye, Edgar." Rebecca smiled as she walked by. "Maybe I'll see you tomorrow."

Edgar watched Lottie's exaggerated movements. Her dangling, skinny arms crept up her sides and rested on her narrow hips. Her eyes seethed through knowing slits, sized him up, and spit him out.

"Talk to me, Lottie."

"What we gonna talk about? The weather?"

"Me. Where have you been...What have you done...Still smoking...Still drinking?"

Lottie sat down on the couch. "You started it. Go ahead and finish."

"Let's see," Edgar said as he plopped down in the recliner, "I went to Charlotte and worked at the airport as a baggage handler; sold cars in Asheville; spent the last year in Charleston working third shift at the paper mill." He scratched the back of his head.

"You left out two."

"Quit smoking three months ago; drunk as a dog last night. Happy?"

"Don't you come up in my house getting smart. I used to change your diaper, remember?" She smiled despite her obvious irritation.

"And you used to kiss Hot Rod behind the barn."

"Lord have mercy. We was only seven. And you wasn't even born yet."

"It was all up and down Salter's Creek Road. You know this town. Probably still talking about it."

"One thing's for sure. If you come back here, everybody's gone be watching you like the *Flip Wilson Show*. Only, ain't nobody gonna be laughing."

"Thanks for the vote of confidence."

"Just telling it like it is." She folded her arms across her chest. "You been by the graveyard?"

"Nope."

"Going to?"

"I doubt it."

"It might do you some good. I put a little bench near the headstone and planted roses and glads. Sometimes I just go there and sit, and think."

"That's one thing I don't need help with. I feel like I'm living inside a movie theater that plays the same reel over and over, only I can't get up and walk out."

She shook her head. "I'm trying to keep my memories, and you want to get rid of yours."

"I got very few good ones."

"Like I got a warehouse full up the street? Sure, I go skipping over there, unlock the door, and all the joys of life come settling down on me like the anointing." Her eyes stared past him. "When I pick up that scent of her soft, baby skin…or feel Daddy's kiss, still moist on my cheek…or hear resurrected groans from the deep bed of night…I rip, and claw, and destroy anything that keeps me from laying hold of them."

Baby's Breath

Chapter Two

Rebecca hurried down the hall to her mama's bedroom. The sun forced its way around the edges of the window blinds and created a hazy glow. She stood by the bed without speaking; one finger poked the thick covers. She leaned close to her mama's ear and whispered, "Are you awake? It's Saturday morning. We're supposed to go shopping, remember? I hope we go to Dairy Queen, too. Do you want me to fix you some—"

"Honey, please stop talking. Let me wake up first." Her mama's face was pale. There were two fine lines at the corners of her mouth, a shiny chin, and dark lashes that rested on puffy, soft cushions under her eyes.

"Sorry. I'll go make my bed." Rebecca dashed back to her room, pulled open the blinds, checked the sky for clouds—saw none—then jerked the bedspread up over wrinkled pink sheets hidden underneath. A dirty sock peeked from under the footboard but was promptly kicked out of sight. She walked to the closet and opened the door. On the top shelf sat Heckle and Jeckle, her Dennis the Menace record player, and three dolls: Abigail, Sally, and Marianne. She arranged them on the floor, where they sat quiet and attentive and looked straight at her. "Girls, you know what today is; I hope you've studied." She placed a sheet of paper and a pencil in front of each student, then paused. She cupped her hand around her ear.

"Marianne, I'm leaving you in charge while I'm gone. If there's any ruckus, take names." Rebecca walked down the hall and stuck her head around the bathroom door. "What time are we leaving?"

"About eleven."

"I'll play school a while then. I've got a rowdy bunch this year." She watched her mama brush her hair and rub moisturizer on her face. "Let's talk first," Rebecca said, as she lowered the commode lid and sat down.

"Okay. I think I'm awake now."

"I've been thinking about how good my teaching is getting with Miss Lottie. I think I just might be a real teacher one day and win Teacher of the Year for Mt. Brayden County."

"Mt. Brayden is the name of our town. We're in Spartanburg County."

"You know I don't know nothing about geography. Anyway, Miss Lottie knew how to read some even before we started, but not very good. Since we've been doing our homework together, she's really gotten smart. Her spelling has improved, too. She gets A's in my grade book."

"You grade her work?"

"No, silly. That's just a figure of speech." She took the open jar of Noxzema off the counter and held it under her nose; it smelled crisp and cool like her chest did when she had bronchitis and her mama rubbed her down with something greasy. "Is Miss Lottie going with us today?"

Mama patted her face with a towel. "I'm not sure. You know how she gets when Edgar comes to visit."

"I knew she was mad yesterday by the way her eyebrows scrunched together. The crease looked like it was drawn on with a magic marker."

Mama laughed. "Hopefully they'll be able to work it out this time."

"Yeah. Well, I'm going to play school now. Oh, remember the plant stake Miss Lottie gave me to use as a pointer? It works perfect, and whenever the students get out of line, I smack the bed with it so it makes a pop sound." She stood and kept talking. "That's what Mrs. Davis did in music, only she smacked her chair with a yard stick. That woman made the skin on my elbows nervy."

After the spelling, math, and reading tests were taken, Rebecca graded them with a red pen. She wished the papers had writing on them besides her checks and Xs. She glanced at the clock on the nightstand. *Finally*. After the dolls were gathered and put away, she rummaged through her dresser drawers for something to wear: shorts, tank top, pants, dress. What she picked out was her favorite outfit which she tried to wear to school at least twice a week but had never been successful. 'You don't wear the same clothes twice in one week,' her mama had said. The brown and white striped pants were wrinkled, but she smoothed them out with her hand. Her white top, sleeveless and made out of a stretchy material that shimmered like silver glitter, was almost too small. She let Mary pull down the front and back of it at recess so it stretched and grew longer. That was the reason it puckered up in places. She smoothed her bangs down with hand.

"Do you want me to call Miss Lottie and see if she's going?" Rebecca asked as she stepped into the kitchen.

"Why don't you just walk over there? I've still got laundry to finish. By the time you get back, I'll be ready to go."

"Yes, ma'am." She skipped down the hall and out the front door. Thick, humid air wrapped around her like a winter cape. Soon the rubber soles of her sneakers heated up and slapped the piping-hot sidewalk; their cadence, mixed with rhythmic breathing, carried her steadily on until she reached Lottie's house. She pressed her moist face against the screen of the door. It smelled like dust and dirt, with a little rain cloud sprinkled in. Her eyes crossed when she focused on the tiny squares made of thin wire. *This needs to be cleaned. Pretty soon it'll be a solid door.* After her eyes uncrossed, they adjusted to the dark living room in front of her. She cupped her hands around her eyes. "Edgar, is that you over there?"

"Yeah, come on in, Rebecca. She's finishing up." He reached over and turned off the television. "So, ya'll going shopping?"

"Yes, sir." She wiped her face with the neck of her shirt. "Shoot-fire-dang, it's hot outside!"

"Go stand in front of the fan."

She turned around and let the fan blow warm air on her back. Edgar sat across from her. He exhaled like he'd worked an eight-hour shift, then rubbed the whiskers on his face. He wore the same light blue shirt from yesterday, but it didn't look dirty. His large afro looked soft, like cotton candy, and matched the shape of his face. Then she noticed his eyes. They were gold-colored like her mama's Frigidaire and washer at home—except with patterned splashes of dark brown that reminded her of an amber necklace she'd seen in Miss Lottie's jewelry box; or was it at a yard sale?

I've never seen a more handsome man. His eyes were beautiful. She watched them glance to the right where Lottie appeared without a sound.

Rebecca stepped closer. "I've never seen you in that dress before." Her eyes traveled up to the yellow crescent earrings, back down the front of the dress, then settled on Lottie's slender feet. "Golly bum! You even got on high heels."

Edgar laughed.

"My goodness, you act like you never seen me fixed up before."

"I've never seen you in high heels. I would've remembered that."

Lottie patted the black and silver hair that swept up in a tight circular braid and crowned the top of her head. "Well, control yourself, because I'm about to put on lipstick."

Rebecca watched. *Pale orange looks stunning against her cocoa skin.*

"Do you want some?"

"Yes, ma'am. I don't think Mama will mind because, good grief, I'll be ten years old in three more days. I'm practically in the double digits."

"Girl, come get this on. You just talk to hear the sound of your voice."

The lipstick was shiny, slick and thick, and formed a smooth coating over her lips. She rubbed them together like a woman.

Lottie took her pocketbook from the kitchen table and her umbrella from the living room closet. "Edgar, I don't know when I'll be home. There's leftovers from what we had last night if you want any."

"Okay. And I'll water the garden later and take the trash out."

Rebecca watched Lottie shoot one last glance at Edgar. A chilled breeze swept over her body. Silent words marched across the room and halted beside the chair he sat in. Rebecca stared at Lottie, who stared at Edgar, who stared back.

He rolled his eyes and shook his head. "Don't worry, I won't."

Rebecca followed the shadow of the umbrella as it traveled on the sidewalk. She was excited about the day ahead. *I wonder what she'll buy me for my birthday. I hope it's not clothes.* She glanced at Miss Lottie's long slender hand as it swayed by her side.

"Miss Lottie, let's hold hands and swing our arms all the way home."

"Do what?"

"Let's hold hands and swing our arms. When we get that going good, then we make our steps match, too. It's fun."

"I'm not gonna do that. There's people all around."

Rebecca looked up. She had never seen Miss Lottie stand so straight or heard her feet stomp so loud. She looked stiff, like Mrs. Radcliff at church. Her head was tilted back and her lips pressed tightly together. *Maybe her shoes hurt her feet.* "When we get to my house, I'll fix you a glass of tea," Rebecca said.

"Thank you."

"You're welcome. And when we go shopping I'm not going to interrupt or ask for anything. Mama says that's a sure sign of being grown up."

"She's a smart woman."

"You're the smart one. Thanks to you, I know all about roses and flower bulbs; I know about hydrangeas, baby's breath, and cucumbers, and squash. Nobody in my grade knows all that important stuff. One day David Fletcher saw a picture of a zucchini in the health book and he asked the teacher what it was. I said, 'That's a zucchini,' before Mrs. Brown could answer him. She didn't fuss at me either. She just smiled and said, 'That's right, Rebecca. Do you have a garden?' I said, 'Yes, ma'am, I do. I got one at Miss Lottie's.'"

"Is David Mr. Fletcher's son? The grocer, Mr. Fletcher?"

"Yes, ma'am. You'd think he ort to know something about vegetables for heaven's sake."

"God knows you right about that, girl."

They stopped at the red light on Main, then crossed over to Converse Street. Matching bungalows, their only difference being the placement of the block steps and the color of the cedar siding, followed the path of stately trees. Rebecca was glad she lived on Converse Street and not Kelly. Miss Lottie's house was so old that all of the paint had washed off and left the wood a dull gray color. Rebecca had seen other old houses on that street that looked worse because their paint was not completely gone. At least Miss Lottie's house was one color.

"Why did Jerome build the high fence around your house?"

"We wanted our privacy. I still do."

"The bad thing is nobody can see your beautiful garden."

They stepped up onto the porch and Rebecca opened the door.

"I know, but this town don't care nothing about flowers or gardens or roses or gardenias." Lottie placed her umbrella in the corner and followed Rebecca into the kitchen. "They wouldn't know a tulip from a daisy."

"Have a seat." Rebecca pulled out a chair for Miss Lottie, then took a clear glass from the cabinet and filled it with ice. She poured dark brown tea and watched it turn the color of caramel as the sun streamed through the window and into the glass; the ice cubes, cloudy and stuck together, clinked like brass. "Here you go."

"Thank you," Lottie said.

Rebecca's mama walked in the room, smiled at Lottie, then patted her on the back. "I'm glad you're going with us."

"Come on Marie, you didn't expect me to stay home with my favorite person in the world, did you?" They all laughed.

Lottie looked at Marie. "So, where are we going? Just tell me it's somewhere far from this rinky-dink town."

"I thought we could go to the mall in Greenville," Marie said.

"Sounds good."

"Well, let's go. I do have to warn you, Lottie. Rebecca's turned into quite a shopper. She likes to look at everything."

Lottie gulped the last of her tea. "Oh, Lord. Maybe we better swing by the house and get my brogans."

Rebecca giggled as she envisioned the chunky brown boots and yellow earrings.

Kmart was the first stop. Lottie realized quick it would not be easy to shop for Rebecca's birthday present; the girl stayed glued to her side. Even when Lottie told her she needed to buy underwear for herself, Rebecca assured her she could help.

"Why don't you buy the kind I got? They have the days of the week on them."

"Child, where's your mama?"

"On the next row over."

"Get your behind over there and stay over there. I need to buy you something for your birthday." Lottie walked away and shook her head. "Help me, Jesus."

When she arrived in the school supply aisle she was able to concentrate. She lingered in front of the pencils, pens, pads of paper, glue, tape, and scissors. Protractors and compasses looked familiar but she wasn't sure what they were for. After carefully selected items were placed in the bottom of the buggy, it was time to sneak to the cashier.

The lady behind the register would have been more attractive without the false eyelashes; they weighed down her already-droopy eyelids. Lottie strained to find her pupils. *She needs curtain tie-backs for them lashes. Is that blue eye shadow?* As she placed her items beside the register she was sure the lady's plump red lips would part soon and form words, but they never did. She paid the lady, begged her to have a good day, then clutched the bags tight to her chest as she fled across the parking lot. She fumbled with the keys and opened the trunk. At last, the birthday gifts were hidden.

Inside the store again, Lottie pulled out another buggy just before Rebecca and Marie walked up. "Marie, can you believe I never found a thing for that child's birthday? I guess I'll have to buy her something from the mall." Lottie sighed and kept her eyes on Rebecca.

"Do they have a JC Penney there?"

"Yeah, they do," Marie said.

"Well, I guess I'll get her some nice underwear and socks. They got better quality stuff there anyway." She suppressed a giggle. "Rebecca, if I get you underwear with the months of the year on them, does that mean you can wear them for the whole month before changing?"

Even through her disappointment, Rebecca laughed out loud.

"Listen, don't give that child any ideas," Marie said, joining in the laughter. "I have a hard enough time getting her to take a bath every night."

After burgers and ice cream from Dairy Queen, they drove to the mall. Lottie still wasn't sure about one large building holding forty or fifty stores, but once she arrived it made more sense. They wandered through Sears and finally Penneys. Lottie pretended to search for the perfect boring gift until they had covered the entire store. Hearing Rebecca's final sigh of relief when they turned to leave—without underwear or socks—was well worth the painful blister on her little toe.

Marie stopped the car in front of Lottie's house a little after nine. Lottie took Marie's car keys, climbed out of the car, and opened the trunk. The sound of paper bags crackling drowned the crickets singing.

"Do you need any help with that?" Marie asked in a quiet voice, careful not to wake Rebecca.

"No, I can get it." Lottie leaned down beside Marie's window and handed her the car keys. "Make sure she brushes her teeth tonight. She ate the whole pack of Bottle Caps I bought her at the drug store and chewed half a pack of gum."

"I will. See you tomorrow." Marie waved her hand out the window and drove off.

Lottie stepped through the yellow glow of the porch light. Her hands were full, but Edgar was there to open the door.

"How do women shop so long?" He took the bags from her and carried them to the kitchen table.

"We don't want to miss nothing, so we look at it all." She plopped down on the couch and flipped her shoes off. "If you're visiting the next time I go shopping with Rebecca and Marie, stop me from wearing these shoes."

"Yeah, like you gonna listen to me. I can see it now: I'm fighting you off, holding your feet and you kicking and screaming with them yellow shoes suctioned on like toilet plungers."

"I'd probably hit you in the head with one of them peacocks on the piano, too."

"That's because you cold-blooded."

Her feet ached; her back throbbed; her neck was tense and tight. She closed her eyes long enough for the sting to fade and her eyelids to think they were through for the night. Edgar's voice roused her.

"You staying up or going to bed?"

She opened her eyes, sat up, and rolled her neck from side to side. "Let me get up from here; I got work to do." She stood, walked to the kitchen, and emptied all the bags on the table. Her stack consisted of a box of pencils, pencil sharpener, dictionary, and spiral notebook. Rebecca's gifts, placed on the other end of the table, were a chalk board and eraser, a box of white chalk, a box of colored chalk, flash cards, two red pens, and a pack of Juicy Fruit gum.

Edgar pulled out a chair and sat down at the table.

Lottie held the pack of gum under his nose. "Remind you of anything?"

He looked at her without answering.

"Edgar, do you know what I got on this table? I got something that's gonna help me grab hold of them memories we talked about yesterday." She touched his shoulder. "God has showed me the way to do it, and I'm not wastin' any more time. Why don't you get alone with Him and listen to what he has to say to you."

"It's been too long."

"If you still breathing, then it ain't been too long." She sat down beside him. "You know, I lost three people I loved that year, too. Now, I ain't saying I'm okay and got it all figured out—"

"Lottie we been over this a hundred times. Just because you throw God's name around don't mean you got all the answers. Why you got to be like that?"

"Because I care what happens to you. You ain't got no life. You got no dependable job or even your own street address. Edgar, you 37-years-old."

He stood and shoved the chair under the table. "You don't have to tell me how old I am.

And you don't have to remind me of the life I don't have. I know all that. Every time I see you, you bring up the same thing. This has nothing to do with 1943. You got that?" He gritted his teeth. "Stop analyzing me. I'm a divorced, wandering drunk. No more, no less." He charged out of the room.

Lottie pressed her fingers to her temples and closed her eyes. *How can he say those things to me? Have I ever turned him away? Ungrateful. That's what he is. And yeah, you right—you ain't nothing but a drunk.* She heard his footsteps return and the sound of the suitcase dropped by the table.

His voice was lifeless. "All I want to know is…where's the God of my mama? 'Cause he ain't here. Not in this house. I would have recognized him already. I made myself believe that one day when I came back, he'd be waiting for me. I guess that's why I kept coming." He paused. "Not to have you looking down on me."

He picked up the suit case and walked to the door. "Mama's God was love." And then he was gone.

Lottie rested her head on the table until her anger flamed, smoldered, then reignited. Her fists, slammed hard against the table, throbbed. "I absolutely refuse to give in to any of his judgmental blabber. That man's got some nerve. It will be a cold, hellacious day in late August before I ever speak to him again."

After a cool shower and a glass of tea, Lottie calmed down. She sat at the table, sharpened a pencil, and opened the blank notebook. Her hand brushed the white page. She breathed in deep and wrote the words as she said them slowly.

Tonight I feel bran new. Like I never felt before. When I close my eyes I see pichers as clear as if they was real. I might not know how to spell all the words rite but I decided I'm not gone let that stop me no more. I'm gone let the pencil do my talking for me. I'm gone let my mind go free and see and remember. Even if my tears wet the paper and my throat closes in tite. Still I'm gone remember. If I don't rite it down then my mind will forget. If I forget then the people I love the most will disapeer forever. They mean more to me than me being ashamed of myself with just a little learnin.

Edgar sat on the curb in front of Lottie's house. She'd never come looking for him. Maybe he would sleep in the swing on the porch. He was upset but he wasn't stupid; he had no place to go. At least he wasn't broke. For all his faults, he didn't squander his hard-earned money, except for buying alcohol. Somehow he'd always managed to find a place to live—even if temporarily—usually a motel with weekly or monthly rates. Sure, it wasn't the greatest of circumstances, but at least he was on his own; not hounded by a skinny Shirley Caesar who treated him like the prodigal son.

"Hey, who is that over there? My son's on patrol and should be by here any minute." The lady turned the porch light off and on, then glared in his direction.

He picked up his suitcase and walked over to her yard. "It's just me, Dovie."

"Well, why didn't you say so, Edgar? Lottie kicked you out, huh?" She stood with her legs wide apart like she feared losing her balance.

"Not exactly, but I'm sure she would have sooner or later; I just beat her to it." The scent of roses drifted from the front of her pink robe and swam around his head. Small white dots of powder sparkled on her skin.

Dovie reached up and pulled the elastic of the shower cap over her ears. The porch light illuminated the plastic and revealed huge orange rollers piled underneath. She crossed her arms. "You got any place to stay tonight?"

"No, but I'm sure I can find something."

She held out her hand. "Give me the suitcase."

"No, you don't have to—"

"I said, give it to me." She took it with both hands and tossed it in the air. "Just as I thought, light as marshmallows." She shook it back and forth, then closed her eyes. "Let me guess: two pairs of socks, three shirts, one pair of pants, and six pairs of whitie tighties. You got some toiletries, too, but that's sticking my nose past the point of welcome." She turned toward the door and motioned with her hand. "Follow me. And I don't want no arguing neither. I don't turn nobody away. Now, if you was to have a gun in your hand or a sheet over your head, I'd have to hurt you."

He stepped into the well-lit living room and looked around; not a bare spot on the walls. Multiple colors, sizes, textures, and shapes competed for his attention. It was late. He rubbed his eyes.

"Lots of stuff to look at, ain't it? But glide your finger across them furniture edges and they won't be a speck of dust found. No, sir." She ushered him around each wall as she spoke with reverence and pride. She was more like a guide at a museum than a nice lady at home in a flouncy robe. "Now, let me show you where you'll sleep."

He followed her down the hall and into a small but neat bedroom with a light fixture above his head that boasted of four hundred-watt light bulbs. "Is it suppose to be this bright in here?" Edgar asked, as he placed his hand over his eyes.

"My dear aunt Willie May used this room until she passed. She was 92 and blind as a bat. She swore the extra wattage helped. She offered to pitch in on the power bill, but I never let her."

"That was nice of you. And it's certainly nice of you to let me stay the night. I'm going to pay you, too. I have some savings just for that."

"I ain't worried about it. We can discuss details later, but believe me when I say—you can stay as long as you need to. I know how Lottie is, and I love her. But she can be as hard as a turtle shell when she's upset."

"Yes, she can."

"I can get boiling, too, but it don't last long. God taught me way back to let stuff go as quick as it barged in." She set the suitcase down and opened the closet door. It looked like a smaller version of the living room. "Oops, forgot. I rearranged my Christmas decorations and what-nots. If you're still here in December, you can dress up like Santa and sit on the porch. I got the outfit already." She cupped her hand around the side of her mouth and whispered, "It fits me perfect."

"Thanks for the offer, Dovie, but I'm sure I won't be imposing on you that long."

"We'll cross that intersection when we get there." Her brown skin glowed. The bright smile on her face never left, even after she offered him a shower and a bite to eat. And it was still there when she said good night.

Edgar leaned his back against the closed bedroom door. *An hour ago I was on the street curb. Now I'm in a comfortable room that's perfect. Except for these spotlights.* He flipped the switch.

He fumbled his way to the bed, took off his socks and shoes, then slid off his pants. Soft sheets were cool against his legs. Moonlight filtered through the open window by the bed, while crickets sang lullabies below. He held the thin pillow under his nose and breathed. Sleep was close, but then a memory floated by.

I had a dream about Mama and Daddy last nite. They was smiling and laffing. Daddy had his big arm around Mama's waist. I saw him kiss her cheek. Then I woke up. I wanted to be a little girl again. I wanted to feel their arms around me and feel Daddy's kiss on my forehead.

Daddy left this world seven years after Jerome and Wy. That just left me and Mama. I sure held on to her as tite as I could back then. As a girl, I used to think she was the meanest woman God ever made. She could tear up my behind. Then when I had Wy, seemed like I understood so much more. I understood more about Mama and life and everything.

It's funny how you can remember special things about a person. It's Mama's hands I remember. Not so much the way they looked but the way they smelled. When I was little and she'd dress me, her hands would be all up under my chin fastnin up my shirt. I'd smell the Clorox. Didn't seem to matter what time of day or night, her hands smelled that way. At first I hated it because it made the inside of my nose burn. She said it didn't bother her and maybe one day I'd get used to it. Sometimes now, I run a little water in the sink. Then I add some Clorox and let my hands splash around in it. And then I smell. Long, deep breaths. I smell Mama.

Camellia

Chapter Three

The summer of '72 ended with the close of Mt. Brayden Community Pool and the exile of two thousand plump mosquitoes. In Rebecca's mind, the only good thing about the end of summer was the beginning of school. A week into fourth grade she and her two best friends, Mary and Patricia, sat on wooden stools in the back of the flower shop. She listened, laughed, and gulped as Patricia told stories about her teenage sisters. When it came to Mary's turn, they hopped off the stools and stood close together so she could whisper. They were so close, their cheeks touched. Rebecca's eyes followed the movement of Mary's lips. Mary's tongue slid between her top and bottom teeth. She thimply created the perfect lithp. She altho had teenage brotherth, henth the whithperth.

Suddenly, the bells hanging from the handle of the glass door jingled loud. They stopped their chatter.

"Who is it?" Patricia asked.

Rebecca peeked through the opening of the calico fabric that hung from the doorway. "It's your daddy, Mary."

"Whath he doing here? I hope I don't have to go."

"Stay back here then," Patricia said. "If you go out there, you know he'll send you home. Parents don't like it when their kids have fun."

Rebecca pressed against Patricia and Mary. Three left ears strained to hear through one small opening of fabric. "What are they talking about?" Rebecca asked.

"I think I heard him say Miss Lottie's name. He did. He called her Lottie Johnson."

Patricia's head leaned to one side as her eyebrows scrunched together. "I thought her name was Miss Lottie."

"You're retarded, Patricia," Mary said. "Everybody hath a lath name."

"Shhh!" Rebecca held her finger against her lips. She saw her mother standing behind the counter with a mad look on her face. Then Mr. Radcliff turned around and walked out the door. "Ya'll wait here. I'll be right back." Rebecca stepped out from behind the curtain and walked to the counter. "Mama, what did Mr. Radcliff want?"

"Were you listening to our conversation?"

"Patricia heard him say something about Miss Lottie."

"We'll talk about it when we get home. Now's not the time. Why don't ya'll go out back and play?"

"Yes, ma'am."

Rebecca set the table for dinner and wondered what was on her mama's mind; she wasn't saying much. Rebecca moved her slices of cucumbers over to where her potatoes were and then moved them back again. The sound of silverware dancing on Corelle always forced her mama into conversation.

"Rebecca, I might as well start at the beginning." She pushed her plate away. "But remember, what I discuss with you in private is to remain between us. If I ever hear tell of you repeating any of this to your friends, I'll wear your bottom out."

Rebecca swallowed hard, forcing the potato down her throat. "I promise I won't repeat any of it, Mama."

"All right. A long time ago Miss Lottie's mama was the maid for the Radcliff family. Mr. Radcliff Sr. thought a lot of Mrs. Dewberry. That was Miss Lottie's mama's name. He loved her like a member of his own family. Mr. and Mrs. Dewbery rented the home Lottie lives in now. Before Mr. Radcliff Sr. died, he deeded the house and the two acres it sits on to Lottie's mama and daddy."

"What does that mean?" Rebecca asked.

"That means he gave the home to the Dewberry's."

"Boy, that was nice." Rebecca looked intently into her mama's eyes.

"Well, Mr. Radcliff Sr. never told anyone what he had done, except for Mr. and Mrs. Dewberry, of course. After that happened Mrs. Dewberry couldn't say anything for days. When she did it was, 'Thank you, Jesus.' She'd say it over and over again. Tears running all down her face. I remember seeing Lottie with this huge grin; her eyes sparkling with excitement. She looked liked she was ready to bust. She said to me, 'We in high cotton now!' I'll never forget the look on her face. I felt myself swelling up and my face lifting itself up to heaven. I couldn't stand it anymore so I jumped up and danced all around the room. Lottie joined in and we just had a fit in the Lord. I mean we had a fit."

Rebecca sat perfectly still in the silence that followed. She was learning to listen, even when nothing was being said.

"After Mr. Radcliff Sr. died, his son took over his position at the bank. That's when Cecil Radcliff Jr. found out that his father had given the Dewberry's one of their rental properties. Even though he was not able to force Mr. and Mrs. Dewberry to sell him their property, he was able to move seven other families off of Kelly Street. And today, Cecil Radcliff III informed me that the city council wants to purchase Miss Lottie's property in order to expand the downtown area. They figure if they can get her to sell, the remaining few will follow.

They're not approaching any of the other families on the street to sell right now because it would be useless to have their land and not Lottie's. Her property is now worth a considerable amount of money because it's two full acres and it's on the corner."

"What will Miss Lottie do if she finds out?"

"I don't know. Why do rich people always want what they have and the little others have, too?"

"This ain't right, Mama."

"This isn't right," she corrected.

"No it ain't. I'm going to my room after I help clean up the kitchen. You know what I'm gonna do? I'm gonna get down on my knees, intercede, and break through."

"What?"

"Just trust me, Mama. Miss Lottie's done taught me all about it."

Rebecca sat behind the flower shop in the swing underneath the large oak tree. Her thoughts were on the dolls and stuffed animals she taught when she played school. Abigail was the prettiest doll she ever had. She sat on the front row. Her blue eyes looked so real that sometimes Rebecca would sit and stare at them, believing they blinked when she wasn't looking. Her long blonde hair curled up on the ends and her bangs were smooth and even. Her dress was made of pink satin and lace. Tiny flower-shaped buttons were sewn on the bodice. Whenever Rebecca spent the night with Miss Lottie, she took Abigail with her.

Sally sat behind Abigail. Her brown hair was parted on the side and held in place with a blue plastic hair bow. She wore the same blue-checked dress she had on when Rebecca unwrapped her Christmas morning two years before.

Behind Sally sat Marianne. Santa Claus brought her when Rebecca was just three years old. One reason she made Marianne sit on the back row was because her black hair stuck out in all directions; none of the other students could see around it. Her legs didn't bend either. When Rebecca sat her down on the floor, her legs stuck straight out in the shape of a v. Some of her eyelashes were missing and the left eyelid no longer closed when Rebecca laid her down for her nap. She wore a real baby's dress that was pink, too big, and bought at a yard sale. Her diaper was a handkerchief pinned with real diaper pins. Rebecca loved Marianne. Even though she was her favorite of all the dolls and stuffed animals, she still made her sit in the back of the room.

Marianne knew how much she was loved. Rebecca told her every day and Marianne understood.

"I wondered where you were. Come in and we'll get a snack," her mama hollered.

The back of Rebecca's skinny legs stuck to the painted white slats of the swing. She lifted one leg at a time and then hopped down. Together they walked through the porch and into the back room that was once a kitchen.

"You were lost in thought out there. What were you thinking about?" her mama asked.

"My students. My *pretend* students." She looked up at her mama. "Any news about my *real* student?"

"No, but we're eating supper over there tonight. I've decided to tell her before she hears it from somebody else. Don't worry. They can't make her move." Mama put her arm around Rebecca and pulled her close.

The smell of fresh-cooked corn and fried ham made Rebecca forget she didn't feel like eating. She hadn't finished her afternoon snack and now her stomach growled. Supper at Miss Lottie's was always a treat. Nothing compared to the flavor of her meals. Rebecca's mama told her it was because Lottie added fatback grease to everything she cooked. Rebecca didn't believe her. Miss Lottie was simply the best cook in Mt. Brayden.

Neither Rebecca nor her mama minded that Miss Lottie cooked supper for them, which was at least twice a week. She had done it for so many years, it was wrong *not* to eat at her house. Miss Lottie said she didn't know how her mama worked all those hours at the shop and still had time to take care of everything else. Rebecca didn't know either. What she did know was her stomach was twisting in knots. Partly because she was starving and partly because she dreaded hearing her mama tell Miss Lottie the awful news.

Her mama and Miss Lottie glided around the kitchen like a pair of ice skaters. They had shared the same kitchen so many times, they each knew what the other one was going to do. Rebecca watched. She knew better than to try and interrupt their routine. She sat at the table thinking and smelling and praying. One thing that bothered her was the way her mama acted like nothing was wrong. She listened to her laugh at Miss Lottie's story about the mole she chased all around the back yard. Then her mama told Miss Lottie about the order for half a dozen Tiffany roses.

"Who needs the Tiffanies?" Miss Lottie asked.

"Jim Robertson's daughter, Audrey, is turning eighteen Thursday. He wants me to make her something special and deliver it to the school."

"I'm sure I got enough. They're a beautiful shade of pink. Don't let me forget to get them out before you leave. Rebecca, can you do that for me?"

"Yes, ma'am." Rebecca looked at Marianne, who sat in the chair beside her. She leaned over and whispered, "It's almost ready, honey."

Lottie turned around with a puzzled look. "Who you talkin' to?"

"Marianne. I brought her with me."

"Who's Marianne?"

"You know. She's my favorite doll."

"I thought Abigail was your favorite."

"No, she's just the prettiest. Marianne wanted to come with me tonight because—well, she just wanted to."

Miss Lottie dried her hands on the thin dish towel that hung from the refrigerator door. "Well, let me see this favorite doll of yours. Why haven't I met her before?"

"She doesn't like to visit; she's shy. Plus her hair is all bushy and I wrote on her back with a pen when I was little."

Miss Lottie smiled down at her. "Why did you do that?"

"I don't know. I don't think I loved her then."

"Let me take a look at Marianne." Lottie picked her up and smoothed her black hair with her rough hands. She pushed her legs down and turned her over, then lifted up the back of her dress. Faded blue scribble covered her back and bottom. "Uh-huh. I see." Then Lottie turned her over and looked at her face.

Heat traveled up Rebecca's neck and face because of all the close attention Miss Lottie gave Marianne. *I wish I'd never brought her.*

Lottie closed the doll's left eyelid. Then, just as Rebecca was about to stand up and reach for her, Lottie lifted Marianne up above her head and smiled up at her. Then she brought her to her lips and kissed her cheek. "I see why she's your favorite," she said as she handed Marianne back.

"You do?"

"Yes. Because ya'll been through so much together. Betsy was my baby doll when I was little. I still got her up in the attic. She don't look as pretty as she did because I played with her so much."

Rebecca looked down at Marianne and smiled.

After supper, Lottie played "Victory in Jesus" on the old upright piano. She softened her playing. "Mama called God's music audible salve. She said that through this piano, healing flowed."

"That's beautiful," Marie said. "I don't think you've ever told me where she got this piano."

Rebecca jumped up from the couch and dropped Marianne on the floor. "I know, I know. Can I tell her?"

Lottie nodded and continued to play softly.

"Miss Lottie's daddy got it for her mama back in the thirties. This never would have happened except Mt. Brayden First Baptist bought a new piano for their statuary—"

"You mean sanctuary," Lottie said. "Go ahead."

"The church voted to give the old one to Mt. Zion Church of God. This made a way for her daddy to get Mt. Zion's old upright without paying any money. When Miss Lottie's mama asked her daddy how he was able to buy the piano, he told her he did some battering—"

"Bartering. It means trading."

"Thanks, Miss Lottie. He did some bartering." Rebecca covered her mouth with her hand and giggled. "Miss Lottie's mama found out later that bartering meant she and Miss Lottie had to place flowers in the church every Sunday for a year."

Hearing laughter calmed Rebecca, but only for a moment.

Her mama got up and walked over to the piano. She rubbed Lottie's shoulder. "It's about time to go, but I wanted to talk to you first."

Lottie stopped playing and turned around on the piano stool. "What is it? Is something wrong?"

"Well, Mr. Radcliff came into the shop. He wanted me to ask you if you've thought any more about selling your land."

Rebecca's heart pounded in her chest. She watched Miss Lottie and prayed.

Lottie's shoulders slumped and her head bent forward; she sat still. Finally, she lifted her head and stared up at the yellowed ceiling. Her voice had no expression or feeling, but it echoed with pain. She spoke like she was talking to God. "I hate this town and everybody in it. I hate them for what they tried to do to my mama and for what they trying to do to me now. They want to remove us—our lives, our home, our memories—like we wasn't nothing worth remembering no how. Rejection cuts deep." She stood and leaned on the piano.

"Is there anything we can do for you, Lottie?" Marie asked.

"No. I just want to be by myself."

Marie kissed her on the cheek and thanked her for supper. Rebecca remembered the Tiffanies in the cooler but never said a word.

Lottie walked into her bedroom. *When you don't care, you don't feel.* A heavy weight settled on her. She felt the blood pulsating in her neck. "I never have understood why you had to let me be born in this rotten town in the first place. Ain't none of them no good except for Marie and Rebecca. The rest of them just care about themselves. I'm through with them. No more." She untied her apron and threw it hard into the corner. "I know I done said some things that don't set right with you and I'm sorry. I really am sorry, Lord. I don't want to hate, but I don't want to care no more either."

She flopped down on the side of the bed and held her head in her hands. "I want to be numb and float like fatback grease on cold butterbeans. I'm sick of trying to love people I don't even like. Now I know I ain't telling you nothing you don't already know. You see my heart. I just got to say it out loud. I got to get it out. I don't love these people, Lord. I sure don't." She unbuttoned her dress and stood beside the bed, letting the dress fall to her feet. "You know, God, if there was a practical way I could love these no count people, I would. I just don't see no way of doing it."

Her feet moved her from the bedroom, down the hall, and into the bathroom. "I ain't trying to be your enemy. Believe me, God." Looking into the mirror, she cringed. "I don't even know why I bother to brush your ugly teeth neither. I been using the same tube of toothpaste for two years. Girl, you just pitiful."

As Lottie shuffled back to the bedroom, her mind traveled through her garden and around every corner and every space of her yard. Years of toil and sweat lay mixed with the ground under her. There would never be a resolution. Her homestead would be viewed as nothing more than two acres of prime real estate. She looked out the bedroom window into the yellow glow of night. The window fan hummed.

Lottie spoke softer. "Lord, I ain't playing now. If you show me a way to love these good-for-nothing, sorry people, I'll give it one more try. I don't want the devil thinking he done messed me up for good. Because one thing I know for sure, I ain't going to hell for nobody. Especially these-well, I've said enough."

In the quiet, Lottie resolved to do things God's way. Whatever that was. She crawled into bed and pulled the covers up around her neck. Tears puddled in the corners of her eyes and rolled down her face. Then, an idea came to her. It was jumbled and in pieces, but still, it was an idea.

Edgar woke to familiar sounds that had traveled down the hall and under his door for the past month. While pots clanged and dishes rattled, Dovie sang. Her voice was distinct, captivating, soothing. For Edgar, it was unforgettable.

He reached for his shirt and jeans which hung on the back of an old ladder-back chair. He slipped them on, then started on the bed. He pulled and straightened the sheets, then rubbed them extra smooth with his hand. He picked up the green plaid bedspread, once on the floor in a heap, and flapped it free in the space above his head. It hovered an instant, surrendered, then gently enveloped the bed. Finally, he returned the yellow throw pillows to their set place, and pulled the shade down to keep out the heat and morning sun.

"Dovie, I'll be there in a minute," he said as he stepped across the hall to the bathroom.

He washed up quick and glanced in the mirror. His face was fuller. He vowed to eat less until the aroma of bacon and pancakes changed his mind.

"It's about time you got out of that bed. It's almost seven-thirty and Saturday morning, at that." She raked the scrambled eggs into a bowl. "Weekend's almost over."

Edgar chuckled as he walked into the kitchen. "You're the biggest exaggerator in the world." He took two glasses out of the cabinet above the sink and set them on the counter. The juice he poured reminded him of the yellow '69 Montego he sold at the lot in Asheville. He carried the glasses to the table and pulled out two chairs. "As usual, you cooked like it's the last breakfast."

"How do you expect to clean these gutters out unlessen you got enough strength?" She plopped down in the chair and flattened the vinyl pad.

"Don't think I'm not grateful though, because I am," Edgar added.

"I know you are." She passed him the pancakes and blackberry syrup. "Tell me about your new job."

"It's going good. I like the people there and the work is steady. The evening passes fast."

"If I had my druthers, I'd be busy and stay busy."

Edgar exchanged the pancakes for the bacon and eggs. When their plates were full, Dovie said the blessing. "For this breakfast before us, Lord we say, thank you for the cook, for the food, and for today. Amen."

"Amen."

Dovie took a bite of her moist pancakes. "I told you a little about my late husband, Howard, but I never told you about the time we had Bishop Mings over for dinner." Her cheeks were full but it didn't stop her from talking. "Howard tried to impress Bishop with his long prayer and fancy words. By the time he got to the end of it, Bishop Mings done fixed him a to-go-plate and was headed out the door. I gave Howard the evil eye because I'd done been cooking all day. Howard says, 'I know you not leaving yet. Not after all them times we tarried with you at the altar.'" Dovie covered her mouth and cackled. "Bishop came back to the table and ate with us. He kept the to-go-plate though."

Edgar put down his fork. "I just remembered mama tarrying at the…"

Dovie took a drink of her juice. Her eyes peered over the rim of the glass. "So do I. Sometimes we'd be at camp meeting until two or three in the morning." She paused. "Now, that snake handling, you can forget that. Thou shalt not tempt the Lord thy God. Enough said. I think it was mostly them white mountain folks that did it anyway. I don't think there's a black soul living stupid enough to pick up a snake." She paused again. "Pick up a opossum—yeah, we'll do that without thinking, but he's got to be dead. Shoot and skin a squirrel? We'll do that too. Still, to this day there ain't nothing better than driving up on a huge turtle in the middle of the road and lugging it over to the trunk. That's the hard part. But later on, that stew's so good, it'd make a fish's mouth water."

Edgar wiped his mouth and laughed. "You could have been Dovie Clower."

She laughed so hard a piece of crispy bacon sailed through the air. "Yea, I'd holler to old Marcella Ledbetter, Ah…shoot that thang! There'd be bits of turtle shell laying all in the road. Me and Jerry would have made a good pair." She picked up her fork and smiled. "I always wanted to be a comedian."

Edgar could only nod his head. It had been a long time since he'd laughed that hard.

Daffodil

Chapter Four

Only one person calls me before six a.m. "Good morning Dovie," Lottie said as she rubbed her shoulder through the thin night gown.

"I'm glad you're up. Is the coffee ready?"

"I was trying to make it, but you called."

"We need to talk about Edgar. Are you going to be home awhile?"

"Where else would I be? Nothing's open at this hour." She pulled the long telephone cord to the kitchen window and opened the curtain. "Come on over."

"Don't make the coffee so strong. Last time it was—"

Lottie hung up the phone. She felt the first smile of the day tiptoe across her face. She filled the pot with water, poured it in the top of the coffee maker, then added twelve heaping scoops of coffee, plus an extra one. Before she made it to the bedroom to change, she heard the loud knock. Lottie walked to the front door and opened it.

And there stood Dovie: chenille robe, matching slippers, inflated shower cap. *Ain't she got some nerve?*

Dovie's smile was smaller than usual, but even so, it spread across the lower half of her face, which caused her cheeks to plump and her eyes to twinkle. "Look, you still in your jammies, too. Kinda like a pj party except it's just me and you. Now, I can have a party all by myself, but you—"

"Does the inside of your mouth ever blister up?"

"Only when I'm irregular. You got some constipation trouble?" Dovie asked.

"No, I don't. I figured the way your tongue thrashes around in there, they got to be some raw spots somewhere."

"Oh, please, Lottie. Can't you be more original than that? You know how many people's said that to me?"

"Why don't you take the hint then?"

Dovie pushed Lottie out of the way and headed for the kitchen. "Get thee behind me, Satan. I'm only here on this earth to do the work of the Master."

"Oh, sit down. I'll fix you some coffee."

"Remember, I like my coffee like I like my men, black and sweet."

"Yeah, me too. That's why we all alone."

"Well, I can't say nothing bad about my Howard, God rest his soul. He was so sweet, ants and bees just stalked him."

Lottie laughed. "You crazy."

"No, it's the truth. When we had a family reunion or cookout, he'd sit in a chair under the shade tree and then I'd throw some of this thin screen we saved from screening the back porch over the top of him. He'd hold it in place with his feet after I tucked him in real tight."

Lottie handed her the cup of coffee and sat down at the table. "Well, you'll be here all day talking your nonsense and I got stuff to do, so let's get going. What's up with Edgar?"

"First of all, let me say he's doing real good. The ice plant needs him for two more months, plus we've heard Tillman Brothers is gonna be hiring soon, too." Dovie blew into the cup, then took a sip. "Perfect. You so good to me, Lottie. Anyway, the problem is, I can't get him to open up to me. I mean, he talks to me and we laugh, but he can't talk about his childhood at all. I know there's something he wants to tell me but he just can't do it."

"I told you when you started this I-can-save-Edgar crusade that he's like that. He's got some deep problems."

"I brought up the subject with him one time. He said, 'A lot happened that day you don't know about.' And I said, 'Well, let's talk about it. You might feel better.' But he couldn't do it. He just shook his head. Why would Edgar say there's more to it than that?"

"Because he don't want to let it go. If he hangs on to it, he can keep nursing his pain with that alcohol."

"Now, he hasn't drank since he's been staying with me. At least not that I know of. 'Course, I'm not up when he comes in from work at night."

"You can bet he's sneaking it in some way. He knew I'd catch him if he stayed here. That's why he was so all fired up to leave that night we argued."

"Lottie, don't you think you being too hard on him? He was only eight years old when everything happened. And he's been so long without a daddy."

"Yeah, and I been a long time without a husband and daughter, too. But you don't smell liquor on my breath."

"No, but you got no social skills to speak of and you block people out like they invisible. And Lord knows, when you think you're right can't nobody tell you nothing different."

"So you saying because I keep to myself, I'm as bad off as a drunk?"

"I'm saying if you got Jesus living inside you, there should be more love coming through. Plus he's a man! You can't expect him to deal with anything like a logical person, no how."

Lottie turned in her chair so she wasn't facing Dovie; her fingers drummed on the table. "I admit I ain't very loving at times, but God knows I told Edgar what he needs to do."

"He don't need nobody telling him what he needs to do. He needs somebody to say they believe in him and that they love him. Somebody besides me. Ya'll family, cut from the same piece of burlap."

She turned back around and glared at Dovie, but her anger dissolved like a fire doused by water. Search lights beamed from Dovie's eyes and covered her with a warm glow. The clock's beat was the only sound between them until Dovie started humming "Savior Like a Shepherd Lead Us".

Edgar packed his sandwich and piece of cake in a brown paper bag. "I'm leaving now, Dovie."

"Okay. Have a good evening," she said as she followed him to the door. "You sure you don't want a thermos to take with you?"

"I'm sure. Somebody might steal it." He glanced at her and smiled. "Thanks, anyway."

The afternoon sun burned his eyes when he stepped out on the porch. He breathed in fresh, warm air. The smell of fried chicken blended with the sound of children's laughter as he traveled down the walkway to the sidewalk and then crossed to the other side of the street.

Mr. Harvey called out to him from his front yard where he looked busy, but never claimed to be; just piddling, he'd say. Bus number seven stopped at the blue house with two broken down cars in the front yard. A boy about twelve or thirteen stepped off first and made sure the three little ones crossed safely ahead of him. Edgar silently approved.

Farther down Kelly Street he listened for Chuck Berry, Ray Charles, and Jerry Lee Lewis. One of them would be blaring on the record player. He turned his head slightly to the left, walked on, and listened.

Funny how thumps of rhythm and jingles of melody can quicken slow feet. The faster he walked, the clearer the beat. Then the piano chimed in and then the voice: strong, punchy, and bold.

Jerry Lee's tearing it up today.

The music carried him past Elder's '76 station and just up to the door of Sanders' Hardware, where he bought a copy of *Mt. Brayden Today* and a pack of Dentyne gum.

"Doing all right, Edgar?" Mr. Sanders asked.

"Yes, sir. Doing fine," Edgar said as he handed him the money, then pocketed the change. "See you tomorrow." He stepped outside, opened the pack of gum, unwrapped a piece and popped it in his mouth.

He continued past the hardware store to the Blue Bird Café, a short distance down on the right. His mama used to send him over to buy a container of their homemade pimento cheese. She said it was the best anywhere. Red plaid curtains hung in the window behind script lettering advertising home-cooked meals.

Maybe I'll go in one day.

He stopped at the curb and waited for the light to change. He crossed over to Spring Street where crepe myrtles lined the way and June bugs lined the crepe myrtles. After he walked another block, Edgar took a quick right and walked up the sidewalk to the front door of the Triangle Ice Company.

The petite receptionist's thin neck surprisingly supported her golden blonde beehive, which was the first thing he saw every day when he stepped into the lobby. She raised her head from the magazine she was reading and smiled her usual polite smile. She never showed her teeth. Her eyes were brown, outlined in black, shadowed in blue. "Afternoon, Edgar."

"How you doing today, Nadine?"

"Just fine now that you're here. That means I only have thirty more minutes left in this place."

He smiled and walked to the side door that led to the warehouse. "Have a good evening. See you tomorrow," he said.

After he clocked in, Edgar placed his lunch in the canteen refrigerator and hustled to his station to begin his eight-hour shift.

Lottie remembered, word for word, the entire conversation. She tried to sit down and concentrate, but it was impossible. She stood from the kitchen chair and walked to the living room.

"You're not going to do your homework?" Rebecca asked.

She sank in the recliner and rocked hard. "Not right now. I got to think."

Rebecca sprang from her chair. She bent beside Lottie and spoke softly into her ear. "Can I think with you?"

Lottie's rocking slowed along with her heavy breathing. "Come sit in my lap a minute." Together they rocked without speaking. Then Lottie's legs began to tingle and her feet grew numb. "Goodness, you put on some weight. My legs done gone to sleep."

Rebecca hopped out of the chair and plopped on the couch. "It's because of all the cookies and lemonade."

Lottie's grin soon disappeared. "I want you to think with me about something. And it's serious and private. No repeating. Understand?"

"Yes, ma'am."

She released a loud sigh. "This morning Dovie came over to talk about Edgar and his job. But soon she started accusing me of being unloving and too hard on him." She made eye contact with Rebecca, giving her time to protest, then continued. "I was thinking maybe you could give your opinion of me. You know, how do you see me? And how have I acted around Edgar when you've been here?" The instant the words left her tongue, she regretted bringing up the subject. *How could I be so desperate as to ask a child her views on adult matters?*

"Well, since you asked, I think I might be able to help."

Dear God, what have I done?

"I'm sure you love Edgar and all, because he is your cousin. But, really, you don't act like you like him very much. I mean, when I was mad at Mary that time, you told me it was wrong to feel bad toward someone. So, I did what you told me to do. I prayed and asked God to forgive me for being mad at her and then I asked him to help me be nice to her again."

"This hardly compares with an argument between third-graders over traded makeup and peace stickers." *Put that in your hair and twirl it.*

"Actually, God might think my argument was even more important than yours because remember how special children are to him?"

Why is it so hot in here? She cleared her throat, casually crossed her legs, and studied her fingernails.

"And remember the day he got here? When I told you it was Edgar at the door, you said, 'Party's over.'"

"That was a little joke to lighten the moment. Can't you tell when somebody's kidding?"

"Well, you didn't look like you were kidding." Rebecca's eyes were wide and innocent, like a bunny's—paralyzed by bright lights. "I think this is a good idea, me helping you think and all. Because there's a lot of things I remember about you that you probably forgot."

"I didn't know you were taking notes."

"I'm just good at remembering stuff. And when you snapped at me, asking me if I was going to take Edgar home with me, I knew then you had some infuriation going on."

"Okay, okay. Stop thinking. That's enough. You've made your point. I resent Edgar because he's a drunk and he feels sorry for himself—"

"Miss Lottie, excuse me, but you didn't let me finish."

"What else you got to say? Repent or you going to hell?"

"No, ma'am!" Her bunny eyes began to water. "I was going to tell you how I see you."

Lottie leaned back in the recliner and closed her eyes. "Go ahead."

"I know you really love someone by the way you get upset when they mess up. You want them to do their best, like mamas do. So, if you didn't love Edgar, it wouldn't bother you when he quit a job or got drunk or moved around all the time."

Lottie continued to rock; her eyes closed.

"Even though you don't like people much, still, you speak to some of them when you walk down the street now. And what about Dovie? I think deep down you really love her."

"Are you finished?"

"Almost. The last thing I think about you is…you look all mean and hard, like a marble statue, but I know you're not. You're more like Play Dough that's been left out of the container, and it's all brittle and crumbly. But, guess what? Dried Play Dough can be softened and I bet if you asked God, he'd soften you up." Rebecca leaned back while her feet dangled above the floor and her heels bumped the front of the couch. She looked at Lottie and smiled big. She threw her hands up in the air then let them fall in her lap, smacking her thighs hard. "Well, say something."

Lottie covered her face with her hands, then rubbed her eyes. "I feel like I ain't got a stitch of clothes on."

My cousin Edgar has come back to town. I wish he'd go back where he came from. He's like a child you got to look after. He's 38-years-old; old enough to stop his foolish ways. I know I got to love him but it's not easy. I was trying to do better then he came along.

While I was at Fletcher's this morning I noticed a man smoking a cigarette while he pushed his buggy down the loaf bread aisle. I got to thinking about the time when I was about 7-years-old. I was outside playing with Betsy and I ran into the kitchen. Daddy was sitting at the table with a pile of tore up cigarettes in front of him. I asked him what he was doing and he said, baby, I'm never gone smoke again. This is my last pack of Winstons. I was happy for Daddy. Mama walked in and said, you got the victory! I don't know what happened but I do remember Daddy having Winstons in his pocket a while after that. Me and Mama never did like the smell of cigarettes but after Daddy died, sometimes we would light one up and put it in his old ashtray. Today I stayed behind the man at Fletcher's and waited a little while in the cloud of smoke.

Chapter Five

While Rebecca developed an eye for flower arranging, Lottie developed an eye for writing and spelling. One spiral notebook was completed and another one started. Lottie also learned that Rebecca loved fruit flavored lip gloss, pastel nail polish from Avon, and ponytails with long ribbons. After all, she was almost eleven. That was when Lottie learned two very important lessons: never ask a rising fifth-grader what she wants for her birthday, and it's never too early to plan a birthday party.

Lottie decided three weeks earlier what she was going to buy Rebecca. It was a large amount of money to spend but that didn't matter. The minute she saw it in the Sears and Roebuck catalog, she knew that was the gift for her girl. What made the decision even easier was the fact that no other family in Mt. Brayden had one. Her need to go to the bank for the money order out-weighed her dread of seeing Cecil Radcliff III. So, by nine o'clock Thursday morning, Lottie was ready to go. Her large hands pulled open the tan wide-mouthed leather bag. She had her savings account book, wallet, ink pen, and Lifesavers. Fortunately, just as she was about to walk out the door, she noticed the piece of paper sticking out of the catalog that was lying on the coffee table. *Thank you, Lord, You know I got to get that money order in the mail today. My baby's gone have the best birthday she's ever had.*

Lottie liked the way her blue cotton shift, starched, stiff and shiny, reflected the warm morning sun. Creased sleeves and flat collar helped hold her head high as she walked down Main Street, while her long, slender arms swung naturally by her sides and fragrant talc stirred beneath her slip.

An elderly gentleman held the bank door open for her.

"Thank you, sir," she said as she nodded. The last time Lottie was inside the bank was four months earlier, at Christmas time. Her visits were rare and short. She never looked around and she spoke only to the teller. And always her head was held high, shoulders back, eyes straight ahead. She stepped up to the counter and began to explain to the teller what she needed.

"Well, good morning, Mrs. Johnson," Mr. Radcliff said. "What brings you in today?"

She turned and lowered her eyes. "I need to get a money order. What are you doing in here?"

He smiled. "I work here, Mrs. Johnson."

"Oh, that's right. You're Mr. Radcliff's grand boy." Her lips stayed tight together as she smiled down at the bald spot on top of his shiny head. "I'm getting a hundred and fifty dollars out of my savings to buy a special birthday gift." *Now ask me if I'm sure I need to get out that much money.*

"Are you sure you want to withdraw a hundred and fifty dollars?" He asked the question slow and loud.

Thank you, Jesus. "Mr. Radcliff the third, I'm gone let you in on a little secret. This ain't the only bank there is and this ain't all the money I got."

He straightened his shoulders and adjusted his tie. "Thank you for the information, Mrs. Johnson. Have a nice day."

With a sincere smile Lottie turned to the teller and apologized for the interruption. "Now, where was I?"

Lottie spent the remainder of the morning raking stranded leaves from behind the hydrangea bushes along the fence and thanking the Lord she only had two trees in the back yard. The fresh April air felt warm as it brushed her bare arms. She enjoyed listening to the birds singing while she gently buried squash, okra, cucumber, and pepper seeds in neat rows between the side of the house and the fence facing Main Street.

After a banana sandwich for lunch, she focused her attention on the large flower beds of daylilies, peonies, bachelor buttons, and lavender. In these beds alone she enjoyed every color of the rainbow throughout the spring and late summer.

Rebecca's voice bellowed loud as she sang the Pepsi jingle and trotted down the back steps. "Guess what happened today, Miss Lottie."

"Well, hello there. What happened?"

"Some of my friends asked me what I was getting for my birthday. I told them I didn't know because I still hadn't decided. Then they asked me if I was going to have a birthday party."

Lottie stopped pulling weeds and looked up at Rebecca. She moved her head over so Rebecca's shadow would block the sun from her eyes.

"Anyway, I started thinking. Since you asked me what I wanted for my birthday, I decided I want—"

"A birthday party?"

"No, a sleep-over, just for girls."

Lottie felt light-headed and dizzy. She took off one of her gloves and fanned her face.

"Are you okay, Miss Lottie? Do you want me to go get you some water?"

"Yes, please."

By the time Rebecca returned with the water, Lottie was sitting at the picnic table in the shade.

"Thank you, Sweetie. Now, where was you thinking of having this sleep-over party thing?" With a shaky hand, she took a drink of the water, careful not to clink the glass against her front tooth.

"Miss Lottie, I've just got to have it here. My friends have been asking me for years and years if they could come over. They say I'm the luckiest person they know; they don't have gardens or screened porches or window fans. Their houses are boring like mine."

Lottie studied Rebecca's face as she continued to talk. She noted the innocence in the girl's eyes and the way her eyebrows moved up and down when she got excited. Lottie watched Rebecca's hands reach wildly into the air, out of control. Then, every minute or so, she would have to move her head from side to side to watch Rebecca dance around on bare feet. How could she tell this sweet little girl that not all parents were like hers? How could she tell her it would be better to have the party at Rebecca's house instead? How could she look into those innocent eyes and tell her that no one would come? She couldn't.

"Can I have it here? Please, Miss Lottie?"

"If your mama says it's all right, then I guess you can."

Rebecca squealed with delight. She ran and kissed Miss Lottie's hands.

Edgar intended to go straight to Dovie's house after work. Guilt weighed heavy on his shoulders ever since his first stop at Leroy's—which naturally led to his first drink. But relief replaced guilt when he realized Dovie would never be up when he got home, anyway. He had been able to drink a few beers every night after work without being discovered. So, when his buddies offered him a ride to Leroy's—again—he said yes.

He sat in the back seat while Raymond Deloy and Oscar B sat up front and talked non-stop. He dissolved into the dark like a vapor. He was lost in his own thoughts when the words "Salter's Creek Road" slapped him in the face and forced him into a conversation he wanted nothing to do with.

"Ain't that right, Edgar?" Oscar B asked as he glanced over his shoulder.

"What's that?"

"Raymond Deloy said Salter's Creek Road don't wind around to the back of Leroy's. He said that part of the road's been closed."

"I couldn't tell you one way or the other. I haven't been on that road in twenty years years."

"Heck fire, Oscar B, we got all night," Raymond Deloy said. "Let's drive down it and see for ourselves."

"If the road is still open, it'll knock off at least half a mile of driving. And gas is about to eat me up." Oscar B looked at Edgar through the rear-view mirror. "Can you pitch in a buck later?"

"Yeah." Edgar's voice was distorted, dream-like. His jaw tightened. *It's dark. I won't be able to see anything.* He closed his eyes and kept quiet. *Even if there is some light around the place, I'll keep my eyes closed.*

"Okay, there's the Holcomb place, then the Stone's house. I used to play over there when I was a boy," Raymond Deloy said. Both of his arms hung out the window like he expected to grab something from the side of the road.

Edgar's throat tightened from the smell of honeysuckle and damp night air. His hands groped for the handle to roll up the window, to block this familiar smell that caused his stomach muscles to churn and his head to pound.

"Hey, Edgar, ain't that your old house?"

He barely heard Oscar B's question over the loud ringing. He glanced out the window at the very moment they drove in front of the house. He had no time to respond—to duck or cover his face—before the image soaked into his heart and etched itself in his mind.

"What's he muttering about back there?" Oscar B asked.

"I think he said something about the curve."

Lottie listened to the birds singing praises to God while the tree branches bowed in reverence. Morning dew glistened like diamonds on tender blades of grass. She sat on the back porch steps, sipped hot coffee, and planned her garden work for the day. Her feelings of resentment toward Edgar normally hung on her but this morning her thoughts were clear along with her conscience. Last night she knelt beside her bed in prayer. She had never been one to extend mercy freely, but she did know that with the measure of mercy she gave to others, the same measure would be given to her. "Lord, I thank you for last night. If I had not met with you and settled things between us, I wouldn't even be able—"

"Hey, Lottie, you outside?" Dovie waved a yellow dish towel over the fence while she peeked through a hole where a knot of wood used to be. "I see you over there on them steps. Come here."

Lottie lumbered over to the fence. Her lips drew up tight like they did when she ate a lemon. Her nostrils sucked in fresh air, then spewed out old. Her thin hands—moments ago folded in prayer—flexed repeatedly as they hung from her long, stiff arms. The birds hushed their singing. She rested her forehead against the fence while her left eye glared through the hole. *You'll be plugged before the sun goes down.* Her eye focused on a pattern of red dots and orange swirls, when all of a sudden a large brown eye with a black pupil and matching lashes glared back. "Put your ear up to the hole," Lottie said.

Dovie turned her head to the side and situated her ear. Lottie's sigh blew hot air which traveled through the opening and tickled Dovie's ear. "Ew, that feels funny," she said, as she pushed her index finger in her ear, then shook it hard.

Lottie swallowed, then took a deep breath. In a kind, even tone, she said, "Manners, proper behavior, consideration. Do you have any idea what those words mean?"

Dovie laughed so hard her head fell forward, hit the fence, and sent one of her rollers flying backward. "That was close. As for your vocabulary quiz, yes, I've heard of all of them and I can spell them too, if you'd like." Her voice boomed through the wood. "You think I ain't got no education?"

The veins in Lottie's neck throbbed as she yelled back, "I think you ain't got no sense. You loud, and rude, and—" She stopped herself, pressed her eye to the hole, and looked through. Dovie was nowhere in sight. "Well, that low down loud mouth's got some nerve, picking a fight with me, then running inside before I have a chance to tell her what I think."

Dovie's unmistakable cackle exploded from the other side. She took one step to the left and leaned forward. "I'm listening, sugar plum. Ol' Dovie ain't gonna do you like a man; I'll listen to you and argue with you all day if that's what you want."

"You talk like we're husband and wife. Lord, have mercy. You're just my irritating neighbor."

"Come on now, Lottie. Settle down. If my eavesdropping was correct, I interrupted you in the middle of prayer. Now, is this any way to act with God, me, and the lilies of your field watching? I think not."

Lottie stepped up to the hole where her mouth fit perfectly. "You a thorn in my side. A beam in my eye. A pain in my—"

"Hold on, sister. You fixing to get down and dirty. That's one thing we ain't never done is profane each other, and we ain't gonna start now."

She knew Dovie was right. "Sorry I got so riled up. Seems like you bring out the worst in me."

"You know that ain't true."

"It's the absolute truth." Lottie squeezed her temples. "What did you want, anyway?"

"I just wanted to tell you to have a nice day." Her roar of laughter bounced off the ground, ricocheted off the side of her house, then pole-vaulted high above the fence where it landed like a jet airliner on Lottie's shoulder, then blasted through her ear.

Lottie closed her eyes. In a voice so low only a deer could hear, she whispered the words of her favorite spiritual: "Nobody knows the trouble I've seen; nobody knows but Jesus." She walked to the steps, picked up her cup and went inside. She began to feel some relief after she sat down in the recliner and sipped another cup of fresh coffee. *I'll just rest my eyes a minute, then I'll get to work outside.*

"Now who in the world? I can't get no peace and quiet." Lottie rolled out of the recliner and trekked to the door. In front of her was the red dot and orange swirl pattern: wide-angled and up-close. She felt nauseous.

"You gonna let me in or do I have to knock the door down?"

Lottie opened the screen door and stepped out of the way.

"I really did have something important to talk with you about. I called, but got no answer so I figured you were out back." She stood solid, fixed; her fisted hands sank deep into her full hips. "I sure am glad we had some laughs outside because what we got to talk about ain't at all funny."

"You the one did all the laughing."

"First, how about some coffee? Better yet, how about some strawberry soda? I know you got some in your fridge because I saw a full bottle the day before yesterday when was talking about Odelia. You know, ain't nothing like that invasion of fizz when it explodes in the back of your throat. Now, Orange Crush, that's one that'll wake the dead."

Lottie walked to the kitchen and poured a glass of strawberry soda while Dovie continued to talk. And talk. Lottie opened the kitchen curtains, wiped down the counters, and took out a package of speckled butter beans from the freezer. She bagged the trash.

"...when she told me she ain't never tried cracklin in her cornbread I knew they wasn't no use in trying to persuade her to try pigs feet. She needs to eat something nutri-titious. Her waist ain't no bigger round than a raw spaghetti noodle."

Lottie swept the kitchen, rinsed out the coffee pot, arranged her dish towels in the drawer from lightest to darkest.

"...and that's how I handle them situations because sometimes people just don't know when to quit. They got to be slapped up-side the head sometimes."

Lottie followed her into the living room.

"Dovie, I'm about to slap you up-side the head if you don't stop talking nonsense. Now what's going on? I know it's got to be about Edgar."

"Let me get some soda in me first." She reached for the glass on the coffee table. "You know you really should use coasters or else you gonna have them ugly white, milky-looking rings all over these nice tables." Her pumpkin-colored lips latched onto the rim of the glass and didn't let go until all the red liquid disappeared. She patted her mountainous chest, then covered her lips with three fingers, which served as a blockade against an unwanted burp. Then her cheeks flared and her fingers pressed harder while her eyes bulged, watered, and fluttered. "Pardonne moi."

"Dovie, you done stalled long enough. What's happened?"

Dovie's shoulders hunched forward. The weight of her chest heaved. "This morning when I went into the kitchen I noticed Edgar's bedroom door was still open. He hadn't been home. I went to get the coffee going when I heard the front door creek. His tip-toeing was quiet but not quiet enough for these ears. I asked him where he had been. He looked down at the floor but never said anything. He sat down so I gave him some time to himself as I finished up in the kitchen." She lifted the back of her thighs from the chair they were stuck to, then tucked her muumuu underneath them. "Every now and then I'd glance over to make sure he wasn't asleep. Finally, he spoke up and told me he'd been to Leroy's and had some drinks. Two guys from work took him there but they were gone when he came to."

"I knew this was gonna happen. Didn't I tell you?"

"Yes, you did. But let me tell you the rest of what happened. He went on to tell me he'd been going to Leroy's after work. He said he wanted to stop the drinking and he told me he was sorry."

"So, everything's okay now. He said he was sorry."

"Well, he started crying—"

"I've been through that with him, too."

"And he promised he wouldn't touch another drop. He—"

"I've heard it a hundred times."

"Listen, this is the part that's so important. He told me he realized last night exactly what his problem is. He said it all has to do with Salter's Creek Road."

"I told you that over a year ago when he started staying with you."

"Would you stop interrupting? You sound like me."

Lottie crossed her arms and rolled her eyes.

"Anyway, he knows he needs to talk to somebody. I suggested going to Alcoholics Anonymous because…don't they do like, group therapy?"

"How should I know? I ain't never been."

"Don't go getting negative, now. I told him I'd find out where the closest group meets. I want to check them out and I want you to go with me."

"What?"

"You heard me, Lottie Johnson. It's time for you to realize that Edgar's problem is also our problem. I'm too old to be looking after him and you're too mean to. We got to work together."

"When?"

"Today."

Lottie unfolded her arms and rested her elbows on her knees, After a moment, she looked at Dovie. "I'll go with you, but listen, my first priority is Rebecca's birthday party, and I got a lot of stuff to do yet. So, if we going, put on some dimmer clothes and take your rollers out; no house shoes; no stripes with plaid. We ain't waltzing up in there looking like we ain't got no good upbringing."

I love the way Mama laughed. She loved to have a good time. She always told me, Lottie, you need to loosen up some, child. I didn't know how to loosen up. I was just me. I think maybe I'm more loose now that Rebecca's been around all these years. She's got a way of helping me not think so much and be so serious. One time she told me, Miss Lottie, you look prettier when you smile, even if your front tooth is missing.

What I remember most about my precious Wyonnia is how beautiful she was. She looked like one of them fancy porcelain dolls. Her skin was the color of light Kayro syrup and velvety, like a Georgia peach. Her eyes were oval shaped. Jerome used to tease me about her eyes, asking me who do I know got them oriental shaped eyes. Mama said Wy took after her great-aunt Florence. Once she said that, Jerome never teased me no more. Wy's little nose was the shape of a miniature rose bud. Her soft black hair hung in ringlets all over her head and her cheeks were soft and plump like fresh biscuit dough. She was a beautiful little thing. I wish I could have known her; seen her grow up.

What I remember about Jerome is the way he made me feel. I remember his manly walk and his handsome face, but it was the way he made me feel that stands out most in my mind. I was Mrs. Jerome Johnson and I was proud of it. Mama noticed that right away. She said, Lottie, I believe you taller when Jerome is around. I guess I was too. I straightened up, threw my shoulders back and raised my chin a little higher. Yes sir, I was proud to be his wife.

❖

Chapter Six

Rebecca's hands held the bright pink envelopes tight. She couldn't stop smiling. As soon as Mrs. Hayes turned around to write on the chalkboard, Rebecca whispered to Mary, who sat in the desk beside her. "I'm giving out my birthday party invitations today!"

Mary's blue eyes grew larger with delight. "Really? Can I have mine now?"

"No. Mama said to wait until recess."

"Rebecca, do you have something you want to share with the class?" Mrs. Hayes asked.

"No, Mrs. Hayes." Rebecca glanced quickly at Mary who had leaned over to put her books in her desk. She was sure she heard Mary giggling. She had never been able to figure out how Mary never got into trouble. Once she asked her. Mary's blue eyes rolled slowly from side to side. She thought for a minute, shrugged her shoulders, and said, "Mama thayth I have the fathe of an angel. Maybe thath it."

The envelopes were quickly stuffed into Rebecca's desk before Mrs. Hayes had the opportunity to question her further. Mrs. Hayes was an elderly lady but, overall, a good teacher. Rebecca wondered how she was able to continue working at her age. "My goodness, Rebecca, Mrs. Hayes is in her early forties," her mother once told her.

Early forties, early sixties. What was the difference? All she knew was Mrs. Hayes was older than her own mother, plus she had a married daughter, for heaven's sake!

Finally, the bell rang and math class was over. Rebecca reached in her desk and pulled out the sacred envelopes. She was determined to keep quiet as she lined up by the chalkboard with the others. As soon as her feet touched the land of freedom she ran as fast as she could to the monkey bars.

Mary beat her there and stood, breathing hard, with her hand outstretched. "Did you invite all the girlth in clath?"

"Of course. Mama said if I didn't, someone would get their feelings hurt."

"True. Mamath know everything, don't they, Rebecca?"

Before she could agree, Patricia Biggers interrupted with a shrill of delight. It was no surprise to Rebecca. Patricia reacted excitely about everything; nothing was mundane. Once, Patricia got so excited about having chocolate cream pie for lunch, she nearly lost control of her bladder. Rebecca noticed something was wrong the instant Patricia's open smile shut tight and her body became rigid like January laundry.

Patricia jumped up and down. "David said you're having a sleep-over for your birthday. Oh, I can hardly wait! When is it? Where's my invitation?"

Rebecca shuffled through the envelopes. "It's right here." She handed Patricia the invitation, then noticed she was surrounded by wide-eyed, antsy, giggling girls. By the time the bell rang, all the invitations were given out, and Mary and Patricia had planned the entire lineup of events. Rebecca had serious doubts as to whether they could possibly do everything they had thought of in one night.

"So, did you give out all the invitations?" David asked Rebecca as they stood in line to go back into the school.

"Yeah. Thanks for telling Patricia about it. She came right over and got hers."

David Fletcher was liked by all the girls in Mrs. Hayes' fifth grade class. Even though he played with the other boys most of the time, he was welcome in the female circles as well. David was a nice person. He was attentive and complimentary, not mean and rude like all the other boys. What Rebecca noticed most, besides his long eyelashes, was how his hands and fingernails were always clean. Once she asked her mama how he could have hands and nails as clean as a girls. Again, her mama proved Mary's observations correct: mamas do know everything. "Well dear," she said, "just because he's a boy doesn't mean that his mother wants him to go around with dirty hands. Mrs. Fletcher is neat herself. So I feel sure that she has taught him the importance of good grooming."

Finally, the school day was over. Rebecca breathed in the thick exhaust fumes from the school bus as she waited in line. The noise of the engine reminded her of garbage trucks; she could always hear them coming long before they arrived in front of her house.

"I didn't know you were having your sleep-over at Miss Lottie's house," David said to Rebecca after she sat down beside him on the bus.

"Yeah. Sorry I couldn't invite you. You know it's just for girls."

"That's okay. I wouldn't come even if you did invite me. Not that I wouldn't want to come to your party and all, but I'd be the only boy there and that wouldn't be much fun. I bet you're going to have a great time, though. Miss Lottie's place must be interesting. I try to peek through the cracks in the fence when I walk by her house, but I've never been able to see anything."

"Oh, it's a wonderful place. Her backyard looks like the botanical garden pictures we have in our science book. The best thing is that we're gonna get to sleep outside. All the girls are bringing their sleeping bags."

David leaned in closer. "Well, if somebody wants you to go snipe hunting with them, don't go."

"What's snipe hunting?"

The bus stopped in front of Fletcher's Grocery Store. David gathered his books and stood to leave. "I'll tell you later, but trust me. Tell them no."

As he stepped off the bus she realized for the first time that David would be a grocer just like his dad one day. Rebecca had a hard time picturing him bossing the bag boys around, but she knew that was the way it would be. When she and her mama went into the store, Mr. Fletcher was all smiley and nice to them. But as soon as they got their buggy, he'd tell David and Billy to do something besides stand around.

It's a shame David has to grow up.

Lottie tried to convince Marie to convince Rebecca to have the sleep-over at their house, but Marie was certain the party would be a success right where it had been planned. Lottie's stomach was in knots. She spent the first part of the week scrubbing the faded linoleum throughout the house. She was painfully conscious of the fact that some white folks thought black folks were not good housekeepers. That never made any sense to her. If black folks could clean white folks' houses from top to bottom and leave them smelling fresh like Pine sol, then what made them think they couldn't or wouldn't clean their own?

Every Friday morning for as long as she could remember, she and her mother cleaned their house. Floors were swept and mopped, baseboards washed down, laundry hung neatly on the clothesline. Bed linens were changed, furniture dusted, and the bathroom cleaned spotless. And now, she didn't need to worry herself with the cleanliness of her house. She knew that. But despite what she knew, she could not stop cleaning until every corner in every room sparkled. She could hear her mama telling her she had too much pride. 'That pride will make you hard, Lottie. Just because your skin is brown don't mean you got to prove nothing to nobody. As long as you know the truth inside yourself, that's all that matters.' Her mama's words pricked her heart as she stopped scrubbing the floor and placed the scrub brush in the bucket. She sat up straight, resting her aching back against the wall.

God, forgive this stubborn pride of mine. You've been so good to me all these years. And now, I can even read and write better than I ever thought I could. I thank you for Rebecca. How she helps me see through her innocent eyes. How her heart believes in your goodness and in the goodness of other people. Lord, help me change, because I don't know how. I don't know how to get rid of myself.

She believed it was impossible to change, but now something inside her was different. Somehow she knew how God's love would flow through her. It was as if God himself came and sat there with her in the hall. She saw pages, words, colors, arrangements. She saw face after face; many she recognized, some she didn't. Lottie basked in the revelation. She lingered, unable to move, saturated with the weight of his glory.

Lottie dialed Marie's number on the heavy black phone in the kitchen and waited for Marie to answer. "The delivery people will be here any minute now, so don't you dare let that child run over here, Marie."

"I won't. She's playing school in her room right now. After that, I'll find something for her to do. She's so excited about the party, I can hardly calm her down."

"She does get herself worked up, don't she? Well, I'll call you when the coast is clear." Lottie hung up the phone and couldn't help laughing at herself. She had never used that expression before, much less seen the coast.

Finally, the delivery truck arrived in front of Lottie's house. She opened the screen door and breathed in deep. The tightness in her chest dissolved. She waved her arms over her head and hollered to the driver, "Hey, you at the right house. Come on, I been waiting all morning."

The delivery man walked slowly up the steps and onto Lottie's porch. His face was rough and leathered but his eyes were gentle. He resembled her uncle HK. He looked at the paper on his clipboard. "Ma'am, it says here we got something on there called a trampoline. That don't belong here, does it?"

"Yes, sir. That trampoline is a birthday gift for my sweet little girl, and her birthday party is going to be right here in a few hours. Come on, I'll show you where it goes." *It sure pays to be prepared.* Thanks to those sleepless nights the week before, she knew exactly where the trampoline should go. It would be better by the fence, facing the road. It wouldn't interfere with the shrubbery or the flowers there. And, Rebecca could see the cars go by as she bounced high into the air. Plus, if the whole town noticed that the first trampoline ever to hit Mt. Brayden just happened to be in her own backyard, then so be it.

"Mama, why do I have to take a bath before the party?" Rebecca brushed her bangs out of her eyes. "We're just gonna be outside playing."

"That's the reason. You're going to be outside getting all hot and sweaty. Now get in the tub. This will help the time go by. We've still got two more hours before we go to Lottie's."

"Oh, I wish I'd thought to have the party yesterday right after school instead of having to wait for most of Saturday to go by." Mary and Patricia had talked so much about the party and the games they would play that Rebecca had little to do except watch the clock tick away time. As she soaked in bubbles up to her chin, she thought about all the fun that awaited her.

First, she would greet all the guests at the front door and show them where to put their sleeping bags and gifts. She tried not to think too much about the gifts because she knew if she did, her impatience would grow. Next, she would show the girls the garden. None of them had ever been to Miss Lottie's and the girls were bubbling over with anticipation. Next, it would be time to eat. Ham and cheese sandwiches, sliced pickles, and bags of potato chips were ready and waiting to be whisked away at four o'clock.

The birthday cake was going to be a surprise, even for her. Rebecca closed her eyes and sighed. She could almost taste the sweet chocolate frosting; that much she did know. There had to be chocolate frosting because that was Miss Lottie's favorite. Even though it was her birthday cake, she knew Miss Lottie well enough to know that she'd never make a cake she didn't like herself. *Oh well, as long as it's sweet, I know I'll love it. Anything Miss Lottie fixes, I'll love.* The thought brought a smile to her damp face.

Finally, the time arrived. Bags of food and drinks were loaded into the car. Sleeping bags, makeup bulging out of an old purse, dolls, Barbies, and games were carried out like royal treasure being loaded aboard a king's ship.

"Are you sure you need to take all of this with you?" Marie asked after counting Rebecca's third trip to the car.

"Yes, Mama. I don't have to take all this inside, but if we need something during the night, all we have to do is go to the car and get it out. This way, you won't have to come back home and get something I forgot."

"Well, thank you for thinking of me." Marie smiled.

Much to Lottie's surprise, all ten girls who were invited, stood there in her living room, grinning and excited about the adventurous night ahead. She wasn't sure how to respond to the girls because she had never been around them. All she had to go by was Rebecca. For some reason she imagined these other girls would be different. "Now, what are all ya'll standing there staring at me for?" Lottie looked around the living room. "Ya'll look like ya'll scared to death to make a sound. This don't look like no party I ever been to."

Patricia was the first to break the silence. "Miss Lottie, I would just like to thank you for allowing all of us to spend the night at your wonderful house and have Rebecca's birthday party here. We've all discussed it and we agree that our houses are…well, they're just not fun. Being here is like being in another world."

"I think that's a good way of putting it," Lottie said. "I hope you won't be disappointed. I've never thought of this place as being exciting."

Unexpected conviction rose within her as she remembered thinking that none of Rebecca's friends would come. Now, as she looked around the room, her heart welled with joy to know that Rebecca's eleventh birthday party was a success. And it was a success in her own home. These young girls were no different than Rebecca. They loved to play with dolls and Barbies; they loved to play school, jump rope, and write in diaries. Maybe some of the girls did dress better than others, but when Lottie looked deep into the ten pairs of shining eyes, she understood the commonness of each young girl.

It was like sorting through the roses at sunrise. She would instinctively search for the perfect ones at first but then be reminded that they were all roses. Some not so perfect, but roses just the same, each desiring to be shared and enjoyed for a time. She remembered her first encounter with the "Touch of Class" rose. Breathing deep, she expected the familiar sweet aroma, but soon learned that the "Touch of Class" roses have no fragrance. They were certainly no less a rose and, instead, their uniqueness added to their beauty.

Loud squeals interrupted Lottie's thoughts.

"Miss Lottie, can I take them out and show them the garden?" Rebecca asked.

"Not yet. First I want ya'll to put your sleeping bags and other stuff in this bedroom over here." They obeyed like eager children on the first day of school. "Now I need to find Marie and my Polaroid. Then we can head out back."

Marie came into the bedroom. "Here I am and here's the camera."

"Okay then. Marie, you lead the way."

Nothing prepared Rebecca and her friends for the surprise in Lottie's backyard. Rebecca's eyes grew larger as she stood speechless in front of the massive contraption. The blue bow was the only clue that it was her birthday present. Then, like a tea kettle beginning to steep, Patricia let out an ear piercing scream.

"It's a trampoline! It's a trampoline! My cousin Jackson told me about them. He jumped on one last summer when he went up north! Oh my gosh! You got a trampoline, Rebecca! You got a trampoline!"

Uncontrollable hysteria infiltrated the camp. It was like a pep rally in a funeral home.

Rebecca couldn't believe her eyes. Not only were all her friends jumping around screaming, but in the middle of the chaos was Miss Lottie! She had pulled her dress up over her knees…brown brogans kicking up dust…dancing…one hand holding onto the dress while the other one waved toward heaven. Rebecca had only seen her dance like that a time or two before, and those times were in spiritual settings. She was shocked. Then she noticed her mama standing by the maple tree, face radiating with the biggest smile she had ever seen. Her tears left shiny streaks down her face and her arms were folded tightly around her waist.

Finally, the excitement dwindled. Donna asked if she could get on the trampoline. Everyone cheered her on. After all, they'd never seen a trampoline, much less jumped on one.

"What's it like?" Patricia asked Donna, afterward.

"It's like jumping on your bed, only better. It's rubbery and squishy! And when you're up in the air, your stomach turns over!"

And so began The Trampoline Affair. Never in her wildest dreams had Rebecca imagined such a birthday gift. She knew Miss Lottie alone had bought it for her. And she knew it was above and beyond any ordinary birthday present. She would always remember this day.

Barbies stayed in their carrying cases. Board games and baby dolls, makeup and jump ropes slept in the car. The trampoline provided all the action and excitement needed on that warm spring evening. The sound of girls' voices could be heard, mixed with The Osmonds and The Jackson Five, well into the night.

The first time I saw Jerome Johnson I thought he was an angel like Gabriel. He had big muscles. He was so handsome I studdered when I got close to him. Then one day he told me I was pretty. Then another day he held my hand. I was seventeen. Mama told me not to let him kiss me but I did. I loved him. A little while later he asked Mama and Daddy if we could get married. They said yes. I was the happiest I ever was.

After Mr. Radcliff gave us our house I thought we were really somebody. I went to Mrs. Biggers dress shop to look at the pretty things, thinking I might could buy a new dress to wear the next time me and Jerome was together. I didn't know I wasn't suppose to be in there. There wasn't a sign. I looked. I heard Mrs. Biggers tell the other lady not to worry. That I wouldn't be in there long because she knew I didn't have any money. As soon as she said that I felt like I wasn't worth nothing. I hurried up and got out of there. Mama fussed at me when I told her where I went. Then she rubbed my head when I laid it in her lap. Her tears fell on my face.

I feel bad now because I got so mad at Mr. Radcliff's grand boy. It wasn't just about the land. It was about how it made me feel. Like I was nobody at all. I have lived here all my life and they expect me to just pack up and move on. Everything planted in the yard I've watched grow and I've cared for. They're asking me to throw away the only thing I know. The only connecting piece I have between my childhood, my parents, my marriage. They almost did me in. I almost let that devil get me. But God showed me a way to love them. Yes he did.

Gladiolus

Chapter Seven

Rebecca and David bounced closer to each other as they rode the school bus home.

"You got a what?" David's mouth stayed open long after he asked the question.

"I got a trampoline! It's wonderful. We jumped on it until after twelve o'clock at night. Mama thinks it's the first one in Mt. Brayden."

"I never heard of anybody in the world getting a trampoline. Boy, that's even better than a ten speed."

"Yeah, I know. That's what I thought."

"And Miss Lottie bought it for you?"

"Yeah. She loves me like her own daughter."

"I can tell." David reached in his pocket and pulled out a wrinkled paper bag and handed it to Rebecca. "It's not really anything. I traded my Richard Petty poster for it. My sister thinks boys will like her more when she tells them she has a racing poster hanging on her wall."

Rebecca opened the bag. "Man! I've been wanting one of these!"

"You know, they're suppose to be accurate and everything. My sister wasn't even sure she wanted to trade but it's too late now."

"Thank you, David. Wait until Mary and Patricia see it!"

"Don't tell them I gave it to you. Me and Mary are suppose to be going together."

"Oh, yea, I forgot. Well, I'll just tell them a secret admirer gave it to me. How about that?"

"Okay. Go ahead, try it on."

Rebecca giggled. "I can't believe it! I got a mood ring!"

The trampoline was the talk of the school the following week. Even the teacher asked Rebecca to tell the class about it. Naturally, Mrs. Morrison turned the discussion into a learning experience by asking the class what made the trampoline bounce a body higher into the sky. Once the students realized they were learning about kinetic energy their enthusiasm dwindled but overall, Rebecca was pleased with the attention. She couldn't wait to get home and tell Miss Lottie about it.

Before Rebecca could tell her the news, Miss Lottie told Rebecca she had gotten a call from Mr. Glenn, the sixth-grade teacher. "He wants the rising sixth graders to come here for a field trip, which would include the gardens and a trampoline demonstration! He said it would be great hands-on experience for the class."

"You mean your house will be a field trip?" Rebecca asked.

"I guess it will. He said it would be near the end of August, just after school starts back."

"Just think, your beautiful garden and my trampoline will be seen by the whole sixth grade class!" Rebecca noticed a distant look in Miss Lottie's eyes.

"Rebecca, I've been thinking about something for a while now, and that trampoline of yours just made up my mind."

"Ma'am?"

"I think it's about time I had aluminum siding put on the house. It does look a little shabby with no paint on the wood."

"What's aluminum siding?"

"It's like they paint your house, only it's better. Trust me, you'll love it."

"Goodie! When are you going to get it put on?" Rebecca held up her hand. "Wait! Don't tell me."

They both looked at each other and laughed.

"Before the field trip," they said at the same time.

Edgar stepped into the kitchen. Dovie stood in front of the stove, stirring corn beef and cabbage. The smell made him queasy. "I'm going over to see this trampoline everybody's talking about. I'll be back in time to eat." *How hard would it be to say I don't like cabbage?*

He dragged his palm over the smooth-topped shrubs in front of the wooden fence. Tiny bugs and beetles flipped into the air like acrobats performing circus acts. He remembered the smell of his hands when he handled ladybugs as a child, and because of their gardening benefits, had promised never to kill one.

I sure hope Rebecca's here so I don't have to chit-chat with Lottie. He climbed the front porch steps, then knocked on the screen door. Their hushed, faint voices murmured in the background. Someone said his name, then yelled for him to come in. Rebecca's vibrant voice and obvious delight at his arrival caused him to feel...welcome.

"Hey, Edgar. Guess what I got," Rebecca said.

"A cold?" He smiled and winked. "Whatcha got?"

"A trampoline. Miss Lottie, your wonderful cousin, got it for me for my birthday."

"I ain't never seen one before. I guess the closest thing to it was an old mattress somebody threw out near our house. Most of the covering was worn through and I could see these rusty springs just waiting for me to try them out."

"Was it fun?"

"Not really. I was barefooted."

"Not many people wore shoes back then, especially in the summertime," Lottie said. "Go show it to him."

Edgar followed Rebecca out the back door.

"I did some trampoline research at school." Rebecca tucked her hair behind her ears.

"I'll show you how to do a knee-drop, seat-drop, and a back-drop."

She climbed on the trampoline. Edgar watched her soar gracefully up in the air. The higher she bounced, the louder she laughed.

After Rebecca climbed off, Edgar climbed on. He bounced and laughed when his stomach flip-flopped. He caught a whiff of cabbage as it floated through the yard and saw Dovie through her kitchen window.

"Don't you bounce off that thing, Edgar," she shouted through the open window. "You ain't got no insurance."

He bounced until his head felt light and his stomach was upset. On all fours, he made it over to the edge. Rebecca climbed back on and they sat beside each other. Their legs swung over the side.

Edgar reached in his back pocket and pulled out his wallet. She stared at the five dollar bill he handed her. "This is for your birthday. Sorry I missed it."

"That's okay. Thank you. I'll add it to the rest of the money I got." She smiled up at him. "When's yours?"

"March sixth."

"Well, when it's your birthday, I'll make you a cake."

"Really? You know how to cook?"

"Some stuff I do. Miss Lottie and Mama are teaching me. Your mama ever teach you to cook?"

He exhaled and looked up at the sky. "Not that I recall. My daddy showed me how to ride a bike and catch fish."

"I wish I remembered my daddy. He died in Vietnam when I was five."

Neither one spoke until Edgar cleared his throat. "I never thought about a kid not remembering anything about a parent. I mean, I was only eight when my daddy died, but at least I got some memories."

"I don't have anything except a tool bag and some tools, a watch, a pocket knife, and his picture on my dresser."

Her words lingered like orphans, waiting for someone to claim them.

"I don't remember his voice or how he smelled. I can't even see his blue eyes because the picture is in black and white. The worst part is when my friends talk about their daddies. Then they ask me about mine and I say my daddy's dead. Their eyes get big and then they say—they always say this: how did he die?" She held up tight fists. "I want to scream, somebody tell me how did he live?"

Edgar patted her shoulder. "Even though I remember more than you do, I promise I know how you feel. I'm 38-years-old and I'm still wishing I had my mama and daddy here." He rubbed his knuckles with his thumb. "I guess we got something in common, don't we?"

"Yeah. That makes me feel better. Does it you?"

"Yeah, it does."

"Sometimes I forget about not knowing my daddy and I feel happy and stuff. But then, one day, I remember and I try to think of a way to make it okay, but there's not one."

"Edgar, dinner is ready," Dovie hollered from the window. "Come on before it gets cold."

He looked at his watch. "I'd better go. I leave for work in an hour."

"Thanks for the birthday money and for talking with me about…you know, stuff."

"You're welcome. And thank you for talking with me." He hopped off the trampoline and walked toward the back porch. He turned around and said, "You coming in?"

"No, not yet."

"I didn't make you feel bad, did I?"

"No. But you did give me something to think about." Her hunched shoulders straightened. "I bet my daddy would've taught me to ride a bike and catch fish, too. Don't you think?"

"Man, yeah!" He smiled big, clapped his hands together, and pointed at her. "I see Daddy's girl written all over you."

Edgar tried not to make much noise as he walked through Lottie's living room.

"You leaving already?"

"Yeah. I got to eat and then get to work." He thought for a minute. "Do you remember the one thing Mama used to cook that I absolutely hated to put in my mouth?"

"Corn beef and cabbage. Dovie's got a plate of it for you, huh?"

He smiled and nodded.

"I thought I smelled it coming through the backyard earlier. Oh, well, you ate it then, I guess you'll eat it now."

"Sure will," he said as he turned to go.

"Why don't you and Dovie have dinner over here tomorrow before you go to work? Rebecca will be here. Marie's got a merchants meeting."

Edgar was surprised by the offer. "Okay. What time?"

"About three-thirty. That's when the bus drops Rebecca off."

Lottie had everything cooked: cubed steak, creamed potatoes and gravy, green beans, cantaloupe, and biscuits. Hot grease and cantaloupe slices shaped like smiles, made the house smell both salty and sweet. The kitchen was warm and comfortable. Dovie cooked big meals since Edgar stayed with her and Lottie wanted to show them she could do it, too.

She took off her apron, folded it, and placed it in the bottom drawer. She caught her reflection in the glass of the stove door. She wiped a smudge of flour from her forehead, then rubbed her finger across her top lip. Fine lines gathered around it like cellophane pulled tight underneath a bowl.

The roar of the school bus's engine drew her away from the kitchen and into the living room. She swung open the front door and stepped out on the porch. The children's voices and laughter migrated through small rectangular windows. Lottie watched Rebecca step off the bus.

"Guess what? Some boy likes me. I don't know who he is, though." Rebecca turned and walked into the house with Lottie.

"That might be good and it might be bad. Are you hungry?"

"I'm starving. For lunch, we had pinto beans and gingerbread cake with applesauce on top."

"Who makes those menus? Well, I got a good one ready and waiting in the oven. Dovie and Edgar should be here any minute."

Rebecca threw her book satchel on the couch, then turned on the television. The theme song to *Gilligan's Island* had just started when Edgar stepped through the front door.

Dovie followed behind. "Hey, Rebecca. Oh, *Gilligan's Island*. Ain't that the funniest show? You gonna have to turn it way down, though, because we won't be able to chit-chat during dinner."

"I'll just turn it off. I'd rather listen to you and Miss Lottie fuss."

"So would I. Just leave me out of it," Edgar said.

Lottie walked through the kitchen holding two deep red tomatoes. "Rebecca, come set the table. Dovie, you and Edgar come on and sit down. I don't want ya'll to have to rush through your meal."

"You know I don't rush when I eat. I graze like a cow," Dovie said.

"Well, I ain't cooked enough for you to graze today, so maybe you should just nibble like a rabbit."

"Very funny."

After they all were seated, dishes of food were passed around and plates filled. Lottie's ear listened for their compliments; she smiled and lowered her head. "It was just something I threw together." She sipped her tea then wiped her mouth. "Rebecca just told me she has a boyfriend."

"No, I didn't. I said a boy likes me, but I don't know who he is."

"How did you find out if you don't know who it is?" Edgar asked.

"I found a love note in my desk It said I love you, do you love me? How am I suppose to answer if I don't know sent it?"

"Rebecca, don't you dare answer that, even if you find out who sent it. You don't know what love is. You can't just throw that word around."

"Lottie, lighten up, please! You gonna have this child warped before she's fifteen." Dovie turned to Rebecca. "You at such a good age, Honey. There's all kinds of fun out there.

Back in my day, we'd roller skate, go to the movies, dance in our bedroom while we played records…you know, just us girls." She dabbed the corners of her mouth with a paper towel. "And yes—I'm sure ya'll asking the same question—I had my share of boyfriends. Most of the girls were jealous of me."

Edgar grinned. "I can see you with a whole bunch of fellas around."

"I can, too," Lottie said, "and they in a huge circle."

"Yes, it was a huge circle for your information. And it was huge because I was admired by so many young men."

Rebecca patted her stomach. "I left just enough room for dessert. I know you made something sweet."

Lottie pushed her plate away and leaned back in the chair. "Of course I did; my famous egg custard. I'll get some saucers in a minute." She wiped some crumbs off the table. "I want to apologize to you, Edgar, for not being supportive of you like I should have been. I'm not making excuses, but around the time we had the fall out, they started on me again to sell the place. But still, I could have treated you better. And when we tried to get you to go to AA and you changed your mind, well, I said some awful things and I shouldn't have. I'm sorry."

His face glowed with a tinge of red. "Thank you, Lottie. Apology accepted."

Dovie's hand clinched the paper towel tight as she dabbed her wet cheeks. Her shoulders shook.

Lottie smiled at Rebecca and Edgar. "I'm an awful stubborn fool sometimes, and the Lord is showing me ways to change. That's why I wanted to start by telling you I'm sorry."

Dovie's moans turned into wails. She reached over and pulled another paper towel off the roll.

Edgar stood and cleared his throat. "Well, I guess I'd better head on out. I don't want to be late." He walked to where Lottie sat, bent down and kissed her cheek. "Thanks for dinner. It was delicious. Send me a piece of that pie home with Dovie. I'll eat it tonight after work."

The table was cleared and wiped clean. The only leftovers were two biscuits and a slice of tomato. Lottie and Rebecca finished cleaning the kitchen while Dovie pulled herself together. The recliner, positioned as far back as possible, lifted her chubby feet high in the air, while bright orange toenails sparkled in the late afternoon sun streaming through the window behind her. She let out a loud sigh.

"What's wrong with you?" Lottie asked.

"I'm wound tight as a broke watch. All this tension I been carrying around because of you and Edgar...it's a wonder I ain't landed in the ER."

"Well, my goodness. You know, we can call 911 right now. It ain't too late. Rebecca, dial 911. The rescue squad will be here in three minutes. 9.1.1. Call it."

Lottie turned off the kitchen light, walked over to the couch, and sat down. Rebecca turned on the television.

"Let's watch *All in the Family*," Dovie said, suddenly perky in the recliner.

"Are you crazy? Archie Bunker's a bigot. I don't allow him in my house," Lottie said.

"I know he's a bigot. That's what makes it so funny. Everything he says is so stupid you got to laugh. What about George Jefferson? He's one, too. Do you watch him?"

"No, I don't."

"Well, maybe you should. You need more laughter, Lottie. Loosen up a little."

Rebecca smacked her forehead with the palm of her hand. "Shoot-fire-dang! We still got homework to do."

Dovie snapped her fingers. "Well, first, how about turning off this light, and Lottie, I'll take a piece of that pie now."

I learned something new today! That Rebecca sure can make my ears tingle. She started talking about how fun the liberry was. I never wanted to go before because my reading was so bad. But she kept on and on until I couldn't stand it no more. We covered every inch of that place. I got my own liberry card and the best thing is she showed me how to use the card catalog. Now I can go and find any book I want. When I walked out of that place I felt like somebody gave me the keys to a gold mine. Any jewel I wanted was there for the taking.

Rebecca was a little embarrassed I think, by the poke full of books I walked out with. But I didn't care. Lord knows that child's made my face heat up plenty of times.

Rebecca has been learning about Haikus at school. That means I learned about them, too. Haiku—a Japanese poem that has 17 syllables total on 3 lines. 5 syllables on the first line, 7 on the second, and 5 on the third. They are usually about nature or seasons. I got to playing around with words and came up with one of my own. I think it's pretty good. I showed it to Rebecca and she liked it.

Beautiful flowers
In the vase add a luster
Of beauty and grace

Chapter Eight

Lottie hated to hear the phone ring as much as she hated pouring alcohol over an open wound; she hated answering it even more. If Marie or Rebecca called, they would let it ring one time and hang up, then Lottie would call them back when she was ready to talk. When Dovie called, she'd let the phone indefinitely. She never hung up the phone. This time, Lottie happened to pick up the phone after ten rings. "What do you want?"

"How did you know it was me?" Dovie chuckled.

"It's almost ten o'clock and I'm ready to go to bed. Talk to me."

"Do you want to go to yard sales in the morning? It's either Pacolet, Pacolet Mills, or Central Pacolet that's having a big one; I don't know which one but we can't miss it. We could ride down Hotel Hill a few times just for fun."

"What about after that?"

"The Apostolic Gospel Church over in Spartanburg is having a huge one. They're gonna serve pintos, corn bread, and slaw for lunch. Plus they're gonna have fudge, cakes, cookies, and pies."

"That's right up your alley. Okay, I'll go. What time you leaving?"

"About five-thirty."

"Lord, Dovie, they'll still be dreaming and drooling in their beds at five-thirty. No. I ain't sitting in the car like a vulture waiting for them people to put their stuff out. That's way too early."

"Well, I don't want all the good stuff to get gone! What about six?"

"What about eight?"

"Okay. You always have it your way. It's a good thing I'm the submissive one in this relationship. That's the reason me and Howard stayed married so long; I always gave in to what he wanted. You know when God starts handing out extra jewels for our crowns, don't be surprised when I get a laundry basket full and you get a couple on a saucer."

"Dovie, I don't care nothing about being decorated like a Christmas tree when I get to heaven. If God wants me to have a crown, then I will, but I ain't sitting around down here designing my costume like I'm going to a ball."

"Do we always have to argue? Let's start calling each other sister like they do at the Church of God. It sounds so loving. From now on, I'm gonna call you Sister Lottie and you call me Sister Dovie. Do you want to?"

"I really don't. What if I try harder not to argue?"

"Once again, I choose to be the bigger person. I'll see you at eight, Sister Lottie."

Lottie hung up without saying good-bye.

Ten hours later, the sound of a horn louder than an eighteen wheeler's caused Lottie to spill hot coffee on her dress as she jumped up off the couch. Before she could make it to the front door, Dovie was laying down on the horn again. *That woman's taking years off my life with each passing day.*

"Mornin' Glory! Let's put this bargain hunting Buick in the wind."

"Just promise me one thing, Dovie," Lottie said as she slammed the heavy car door. "When somebody has a dime marked on something, don't ask them if they'll take a nickel."

"Well, my goodness. That's taking all the fun out of it. If it ain't a bargain, I don't want it."

"You got all them Avon bottles and salt and pepper shakers stacked up to the ceiling now. I really don't know why you keep going to yard sales anyway. Where you gonna put the stuff you buy today?"

"I'll find a place. Them Avon bottles are gonna be worth hundreds of dollars in about thirty years."

"You won't be alive in thirty years!"

"How do you know? My granny lived to be 98 and my mama was 94 when she died."

"And how old are you now, Dovie?"

"Sixty-two-ish"

"Well, okay. When you turn ninety-two-ish you'll be able to cash in your Avon bottles to pay for another week at the old folk's home."

"Sister Lottie, your negativism ain't at all attractive."

Lottie started keeping at least two flowers from each order she received from Marie. She was also asking Marie who ordered what and for what occasion. If Marie was curious about all the questions, she never mentioned it.

Lottie glanced at the clock on the stove. She jumped up from the table, rinsed her hands, then hurried down the hall to her bedroom. She threw the shoe boxes on the top shelf of the closet, slammed the door, then stood firmly in front of it.

"What did you just put in the closet?" Rebecca asked.

Lottie batted her eyes and spoke softly. "Do what?"

"I saw you putting something up like you were trying to hide it from me."

Rebecca's determined expression only caused Lottie's defenses to stiffen more. "Well, first of all, I'm a grown-up and grown-ups can hide things if they want to, without giving children an explanation. Second, this is my house and just where did you come from?" She gave Rebecca a sly smile.

"I'm sorry. I just got off the bus and I ran in."

"All right now. No more rude questions. If I'd ever asked my mama or daddy what they was doing or why they was doing it, they would have marched me behind the garden shed; and not for no flower bulb lesson."

"Oh, I know what you're talking about, believe me. Mama acts all sweet around you, but have you ever seen her mad? She's scary."

"Rebecca, your mama's not scary. I think what you mean is you respect your mama and her rules. That's the way it should be. She's only looking out for your good. Don't you know that?"

"I guess so. But one day she told me she was going to beat the fire out of me. I was so scared my knee caps quivered."

"Oh my goodness! And just what did you do to make her say such a thing?"

Rebecca dropped her head. "I'd rather not say."

"Okay then. I've known your mama all my life and she ain't got a mean bone in her body. I'm just guessing, but it must have been something pretty bad for your mama to say that."

"Yes, ma'am. It was. I noticed you said ain't in your sentence and you told me to remind you not to say that anymore."

Lottie cleared her throat. "Thank you for the reminder." She realized she still had her hand on the closet door. *Maybe I should tell her about the flowers.* But before she did anything, she asked Rebecca about the homework assignment.

"We don't have any. I guess that means we can jump on the trampoline until supper."

"Girl, you got to remember I ain't—I mean, I'm not as young as you. I been around the block a few times."

"About fifty-four times. You told me."

"Oh, Lord, help me not to strangle this child. T-a-c-t. Even an uneducated black woman knows that word and how to spell it. Ever heard of it?"

"No, ma'am. I'm just speaking the truth in love. Isn't that what you talked to me about the other day?"

"Yes, but that's not exactly what I meant." Her long rough fingers pinched Rebecca's round cheek.

"Ouch! That hurt!"

"I meant for it to. Now do you want to see what's in the closet or not?"

"I sure do."

"First, go wash your hands and make sure they're extra clean."

Lottie arranged the white pages in rows on the bed. She told Rebecca to step closer when she returned from washing her hands.

"Did you paint these flowers?"

"No, I pressed them. Have you ever heard of flower pressing?"

"No, ma'am."

"Well, I heard tell of it years ago. Aunt Edith, uncle HK's wife, used to press flowers from her garden and she showed me how. I never did anything with it though, not until last month."

"How come you never told me?"

Lottie saw the hurt in Rebecca's eyes. "Well now, let me tell you how it all came about first. I was just experimenting with it really. It wasn't until you took me to the liberry that I was able to get a book and read up on it."

"Excuse me, Miss Lottie, but it's library, not liberry. Lots of people at my school say that and I did too when I was little, but then I found out the real pronunciation. So, it's library. I hope I used tact."

"Yes, you certainly did, and I appreciate you telling me. Library. I like the way that sounds. Kind of like Brer Rabbit in the old Uncle Remus stories. Sure does. Anyway, let me start at the beginning of the whole thing so you can understand where I'm coming from on all this because, believe me, it wasn't no great idea I come up with. It was the Lord's doing. Do you remember when I got all upset about Mr. Radcliff's grand boy wanting me to move?"

"Yes, ma'am."

"I was so upset that night that I had it all out with the Lord. I knew then he had something special for me to do, but I didn't know what. Then, a while later, he gave me the idea. He just dropped it in my spirit kind of like dumplings being dropped in chicken broth. He told me, 'Lottie, since you asked me to show you a way to love the people of Mt. Brayden, here it is. Each time Marie places an order for someone's special occasion, I want you to keep one or two of the flowers for pressing. Then I want you to write who the flowers were for, who they were from, for what event, and the date.'"

Rebecca sat on the bed speechless; her legs crossed in front of her.

"So, that's what I've been doing. I went to the library and found a good book on flower pressing. I've been keeping notes and everything. I'm a little embarrassed because I'm keeping track of the whole town's business. I'd usually call it meddling, but that don't seem like the right thing to call it now, knowing the spiritual circumstances and all."

"Oh, I don't think it's meddling at all, Miss Lottie. It's more like you're just following commandments. You'd be crazy not to listen to God."

"I know that's right."

"Whew, all done!" Rebecca said. She closed her math book.

"We didn't have as much as we did yesterday, did we?" Lottie asked.

"No, ma'am. That's because we had a substitute teacher today. Oh, I forgot to tell you. Guess who's going to have a baby."

"Who?"

"Mr. and Mrs. Radcliff."

"Are you sure?"

"Yes, ma'am. Mary told the whole class yesterday, and at recess she told us how her mama and daddy were surprised. No, she said shocked. She said her brother is so embarrassed that he told his parents he wants to go to night school. He's a senior."

"Well, I knew he was a teenager, but I didn't know he was that old."

"Mary said her mama told her that she wasn't prepared to be a mama again, that Mary was supposed to be the last child."

"I guess God had other plans, then. Give Mrs. Radcliff some time and she'll be happy about it," Lottie said.

"I don't know if she will or not. Mary said all she does is cry."

"I don't understand it. No baby's birth has ever surprised God. He's the one who created the child in the first place. She should be crying tears of joy instead of tears of sadness."

Lottie straightened her papers and placed them inside her notebook. She decided now would be a good time to find out what Rebecca knew about the birds and the bees. Since she was going into the sixth grade, Lottie wanted her to hear *that* truth from an adult instead of from a bunch of silly girls. "Rebecca, has your mama talked to you about, the uh, birds and the bees?" Lottie smoothed the front of her dress with damp palms.

"She told me about the birds and the bees *and* the flowers and the trees!" Rebecca smiled and folded her arms; then she winked.

"Thank God." Lottie sighed.

"Do you want to talk about it, too? Because if you do, I don't mind. Mama said it's just a part of life and growing up."

"Yes, but understand that most of that information is for the grown-up part of your life and not for now. It's more like for-your-information-only."

"I know. We say FYI."

"That's right. So, now that we've settled all that, how about some brownies?"

"Groovy!"

The rest of the afternoon Lottie showed Rebecca how to make creamed potatoes, cut, batter and fry okra, and how to make the perfect gallon of tea. "My grandma used to make her tea like this. She showed my mama, my mama showed me and —"

"You're showing me."

"Yes, because you're the daughter I didn't get to raise. Now, the secret to smooth, dark tea is in here." Lottie opened the worn cabinet door and took out a small yellow box. "This is baking soda. After the tea comes to a boil, you turn the burner off and add two pinches of the baking soda. Then put a lid on the pot and let it sit for about ten minutes."

"Oh, I'll be sure to remember that because Patricia brags on her mama's tea all the time. She swears up and down that the secret to good tea is in the Luzianne tea bags her mama uses."

Lottie was quick to correct Rebecca. "Don't use the word swear. That's not right."

"I didn't say I swear to God or anything."

"I know. If you'd said that I'd really got hold of you. The Bible says we're not to swear by heaven because it's God's throne and we're not to swear by earth because it's God's footstool. Let your yes be yes and your no be no."

"Yes, ma'am," Rebecca said, eager to change the subject. "Are you excited about having your home aluminum-sided soon, Miss Lottie?"

"Child, I'm so excited I haven't been able to sit still all day. It was all I could do to get through that homework."

"That's the way I was when I had my sleep-over."

"They said it takes a good week to do it all, so I'm gonna try to be patient. I thought I might do some extra flower pressing during the day to keep my mind off them being here. They'll be in my way out in the yard. They better not step on any of my flowers either."

"Miss Lottie, I'm reminding you to be positive."

"Thank you, dear. But if they don't stay on the pathways, they'll mess up my flowers and if they do, I'm positive they gonna be taking money off my bill."

Saturday mornings in the back room of the florist shop turned into the gathering place for Rebecca, Mary, and Patricia. They would catch up on the latest in school news like who was liking who and what grades they made on tests that week.

"When we have our field trip to Miss Lottie's house, will we be able to jump on the trampoline?" Mary asked Rebecca.

"I guess so. Mr. Glenn said it would be educational. Just standing around looking at it wouldn't teach us nothing."

Patricia sat at the table listening and watching Rebecca cut rose stems. "Mary, is your mama still crying about having a baby?"

"No. She stopped crying Thursday night. Daddy told her to go shopping in Greenville on Friday and that seemed to make her feel better."

"I wish you'd have another sleep-over, Rebecca. Do you think you could ask Miss Lottie?"

"Patricia, that's the third time you've asked me. Mama said I have to wait until Miss Lottie suggests it. You know how grown-ups are. They never like for kids to ask for anything."

"That's the truth," Mary said. "I never just come right out and ask for anything. I hint around and somehow my parents figure out what I want and then they get it for me."

Rebecca was still adjusting to Mary's unlisped words. "Well, Miss Lottie doesn't take to hinting around. She'd see through that in a minute. And most kids don't get everything they want like you do, Mary." Rebecca had wanted to tell both Mary and Patricia that for a long time. The words seemed to tumble out of her mouth before she had time to think about it.

"Thanks a lot, Rebecca. Don't forget I'm about to go from being the baby in the family to being next-to-last. And for your information, I don't get everything I want. I told Mama last week how nice it would be to listen to Donny Osmond at night while I fall asleep. But do I have an eight-track tape player yet? No, I don't."

"When you do, will you invite me over so I can listen to Donny?" Patricia asked nicely.

"Sure, maybe next week."

Rebecca stood with her hands on her hips. "See?"

"See what? You got a trampoline. The only one in the whole slice-of-pie-shaped state of South Carolina. You can't say nothing about me and Patricia getting our way all the time."

Mary's words stung Rebecca's ears. "I think it's time for me to clean out the cooler and after that I have to sweep off the sidewalk," she said hurriedly.

"Well, you don't have to get in a huff. Besides, me and Patricia's got stuff to do, too. Don't we?"

"Like what?" Patricia asked.

"Shut up and come on." Mary stormed out with Patricia in tow.

Why am I friends with them? Rebecca's thoughts wandered as she swept cigarette butts and candy wrappers off the sidewalk. The sun beamed down on her bare arms. *Did I put on deodorant like Mama said?*

Marie tapped on the plate glass window from inside the shop.

"Yes, Mama?" Rebecca opened the door and stepped inside.

"Honey, if you're finished, you can go over to Lottie's. She said she has some pressing news to tell you, whatever that means."

Rebecca laughed as she ran to put the broom in the back room. *She has a clever way with words.* She yelled good-bye to her mama as she ran through the shop and out the front door.

Minutes later, Rebecca stood in Miss Lottie's living room. "Pressing news? That's a good one."

"I thought you'd like that. Sorta like code. Listen, what took you so long? I been waiting over five minutes."

"You sure are impatient, Miss Lottie."

"I know it, but I started pressing some flowers and I wanted you to watch." She turned to go back into the kitchen. "Follow me." Miss Lottie led the way to the back porch where the flower press sat on top of the porcelain table.

"It's really easy, Rebecca. I made the press out of two pieces of plywood and a few bricks to lay on top. First, you pick out the flowers you want to press. Carefully lay them between two paper towels and place them on the plywood. Put the other piece of plywood on next, then the bricks go on top of that. All the weight presses the moisture out of the flowers."

"That looks easy," Rebecca said, eager to press her first flower. "Can I try one?"

"Yes. I just cut them before you got here. That's another reason I wanted you to hurry over."

Rebecca's hand quickly plucked the stem from the mason jar. "I love violets! Did I tell you Mama bought me a cape with violets embroidered between the buttons?"

"No, you didn't. Sounds beautiful. All right now, cut a little of the stem off and lay the flower on the paper towel. Here, take these tweezers and arrange the petals so they look their best."

Rebecca carefully moved the petals until they were arranged like she wanted them. "Now I put a paper towel on top?"

"Well, go ahead and arrange some more flowers on there so we don't waste the space.

You can get a lot more flowers on this sheet." Lottie rested her hand on Rebecca's shoulder. "I sure am glad you like this. I think florists and gardeners should know how to preserve their beautiful treasures, and what better way than this? Okay, after two or three days, you'll check the paper towels to see if they're damp. If they are, replace them. Then put the plywood and bricks back on top. It takes a good two weeks for the flowers to dry all the way."

"What do you do with the flowers then?" Rebecca asked.

"I usually store them in Tupperware until I'm ready to make my memory cards. Come to the bedroom and I'll show you some." They walked together down the hallway to Lottie's bedroom. Lottie squatted down beside the old iron bed and reached underneath, pulling out a large shoe box. "Let's see." She took off the lid. "Here's one. What do you think?" She handed the card to Rebecca.

"The flowers are beautiful, but they're not as colorful as real flowers."

"They lose some of their color. Now, turn it over."

Rebecca read the words out loud. "Date: May 17, 1974. Occasion: Rebecca's Birthday Sleep-over. Flowers: Violets and Daffodils. Memory: These flowers were in the cut glass vase on top of the piano at Lottie's house. They may not have been noticed because of the bigger memory maker in the backyard—a trampoline. The only one in Mt. Brayden."

She looked at Miss Lottie and smiled. "My special day will live forever because of this beautiful card you made." She leaned over and kissed her gently on the cheek.

Just when I started to think Edgar was improving, this happened. My stomach feels queasy and my hands haven't stopped shaking since two days ago. I've just now been able to write about it.

Rebecca wanted to go with me to the cemetery and help change out the flowers. I go every Sunday. She hadn't been in a month or so and she was looking forward to it. She toted the water pitcher and the flowers. I carried my heavy tote bag.

The sun was hot, so we stopped by the Elder's '76 station and drank a Pepsi with peanuts. Then we walked on to the gravesites. The monkey grass around the square lot formed a beautiful border. The tulips we planted last year were standing tall and strong. Rebecca headed straight for the spigot beside the church steps and filled the pitcher with water. I sat on the bench beside the large cedar tree. This was my Sunday visit with my family. I lingered patiently in the sounds, smells, and memories that live there.

After Rebecca replaced the vase with fresh water and Zinnias, I rummaged through my bag and dug out the wind chime. I hung it from the usual branch then sat back down on the bench with Rebecca. We listened to the tinkling of the metal rods as they danced with each other in the breeze. Rebecca asked about Wy's favorite baby toy, when she learned to walk, and what words she could say. Then we imagined what she would be today— how many children she'd have, if she was a teacher or secretary or nurse. We laughed and shed a few tears. My family was alive in my heart.

Then Bishop Clemmons pulled up in the parking lot. I saw him biting the side of his cheek and heard him jingling his keys in his pocket as he walked toward us. He lowered his head. He asked if it was okay to discuss a private matter with me even though Rebecca was there. I told him to go ahead and say what he needed to say. It happened after I left church and headed back home. Most of the congregation was still talking in the parking lot or standing by their cars. He told me Edgar spent the night here, on sacred ground—the resting place of my loved ones—drunk. He woke up just in time to stumble across the parking lot and make a fool of himself in front of most of the church members. Bishop Clemmons was kind enough to put Edgar in his car and drive him to Dovie's. He stopped by my house to tell me, but I had already left for the cemetery.

Bishop put his hand on my shoulder and told me not to take it too hard, that every family has embarrassing moments with family members. But this was more than just an embarrassing moment. After he left, I walked behind the tombstones, picked up the empty bottles and put them in my tote. Then I walked behind where Mama and Daddy lay and over to the old oak tree. Aunt Edith and uncle HK slept there. I picked up the other bottles and the folded note left partially stuck under the crack between the headstone and the cement foundation.

I didn't read the note. I'd read them before; I'd picked up the bottles before; I had been embarrassed, humiliated and sickened before. But this was the first time Rebecca had experienced it. She cried. It was the first time the church congregation had witnessed Edgar's shameful behavior, too. Is the story still burning up the phone lines?

It has been two days and I still have not cried. It's happened too many times before.

Chapter Nine

Edgar finished making the coffee and wiped down the counter. He stopped by Krispy Kreme on his way home last night and bought a dozen fancy doughnuts. He thought he'd surprise Dovie this morning.

"Edgar Dewberry, look what you done went and did." Her smile was broad and open and black behind pearly white teeth. Her eyes flashed the reflection of the window in front of her; they sparkled.

"I knew you liked fancy doughnuts, so here's a whole dozen. Eat until you can't eat anymore."

"Aw, I can only eat one. You know I'm suppose to be watching my weight. You still gonna fix the car?"

"Yeah. I was on my way out to the shed to look for the tools. I hope you got what I need."

Dovie opened the window above the sink, then sat down at the table. "I should; Howard did all our maintenance. Except for the time I drove too fast over a pothole and busted the radiator all to bits. He was so mad at me. I kept driving it until I got home. The thing was smoking like a gully full of burning leaves. He'd say, you got to slow down, woman. You tearing up stuff faster than I can fix them."

"Well, I don't think this is your fault. Alternators give out after so long. I'm going to look for the tools."

He walked back to the house a minute later to get a flashlight. From the back door he saw Dovie sitting at the table staring at the doughnuts. He couldn't resist—he watched her.

She sat at the table with a large cup of steaming coffee and one doughnut. She took the knife and cut the doughnut into tiny pieces, which she savored, slow and with passion. The yellow lemon jelly oozed out onto the plate and stayed there until she wiped her finger through it and then sucked it off. She rolled her eyes, closed her eyelids, and moaned. She finished, wiped her hands, and slid the plate away.

He was impressed by her will power and determination.

Then she pushed her chair back, stood, and crept quietly over to the box on the counter. She held her hands in front of her and wriggled all her fingers around like they wanted to jump in the box and swim with the doughnuts. His faith began to slip. Evidently, she couldn't decide which one to eat next, so she carried the entire box back to her seat, sat down, and plunged in.

Edgar couldn't decide which made him feel worse: buying Dovie the doughnuts or spying on her.

Lottie was glad for the time she, Marie, and Rebecca had together on this beautiful Saturday afternoon. They sat around the cement picnic table in the back yard eating homemade peach ice-cream. Saturdays were the only real day the three of them had to do whatever they wanted to do; with the exception of Marie, who sometimes had weddings to take care of.

"What's going on at Dovie's?" Marie asked.

Lottie huffed. "She told me Edgar was going to fix her car today. That is, if he's sober."

"What's wrong with it?" Rebecca wiped the dribble from her chin.

"I don't know. It was running fine last Saturday when we went to the peach shed. Lord have mercy, did I ever tell ya'll about that?"

"No," Rebecca and Marie said in unison.

"Well, me, Dovie, and Clovis drove over to the peach shed in Chesnee. We had a good time, even though Dovie talked the whole way there and back. I couldn't help but laugh when I'd look over at her. She was hunched over the steering wheel like somebody was gonna come along and steal it away from her. Her bright orange fingernails reflected the sun when she tapped them on the dashboard from time to time. Lord, she had the music up so loud I couldn't even hear Clovis in the backseat. So, there we were barreling down the road like a bowling ball covered in Crisco. The windows were down because Dovie wanted to save on gas, so we all had our heads wrapped up in scarves, looking like three Aunt Jemimas just escaped from a low-country plantation." Lottie gripped an imaginary steering wheel and bounced up and down.

"When we pulled in the gravel parking lot, the car filled up with white, silvery dust. I tried to fan it away from my face but it didn't do no good; we were covered in it. Of course, Me and Clovis were under the peach shed before Dovie removed all of herself from the car. Then she comes bouncing to the shed chanting an old jingle we used to say when we were kids. 'Shew, shew, I smell peaches, here comes Lottie with a hole in her britches.' I just shook my head and acted like my name wasn't Lottie. Everybody there knew we was together though, because of our wrapped-up heads. There wasn't no getting around that."

Lottie took the last bite of her ice cream.

"We all bought us a bushel of peaches for canning, jellies, and pies. And this good ice-cream we're eating. Clovis bought

some boiled peanuts. We ate them on our way back home."
Lottie folded her arms across her chest and let out a sigh.
"I kind of felt like I was a young, carefree girl. It was fun.
I thanked Dovie for the ride when we got back home. She
smiled and gave me a big hug."

Lottie laughed hard. "Oh, me. That is one massive woman."

The young man looked up from his clipboard. "Yes, ma'am,
Mrs. Johnson. We'll have your house finished by the end of
the week."

"Good," Lottie said, looking eye to eye with what appeared
to be a young man no older than twenty. His dark black hair
and long sideburns made his complexion look more pale and
his dark blue eyes more penetrating and unforgettable. "I've
got a class of sixth graders coming over for a field trip a week
from Friday. I've got to have the house finished and the yard
picked up good."

"You don't have to worry about that. We'll be out of here
by Friday, and your house will look better than the day it was
built," he said.

Of course, they didn't have the house finished by Friday.
It was late Wednesday afternoon before the last piece of
aluminum scrap and the old windows were loaded into the
back of a rusty white Ford pickup. Lottie let the curtain fall
back in its place and huffed. "Yeah. And what if I didn't push
them to start with? They'd still have the whole place a wreck
and me suppose to have twenty-something people over here
looking at flowers, stepping over aluminum scrap, and saw
horses, and-all-and-everthang." She walked from her bedroom
through the living room and answered the knock at the door.

"We're all finished, Mrs. Johnson," the young man said. "Sorry it took us a little longer than we expected. When did you say the kids were coming?"

"Since today's the sixteenth, that means they'll be here in two days." She was unable to hide her frustration. "Are you sure everything is picked up?"

"Yes, ma'am. Would you like to go outside and look the job over?"

"I believe I will. Thank you." She walked through the door and down the concrete steps.

When she got as far away from the house as she could, she turned around to see the finished work. Lottie stood frozen; she was speechless.

"Well, what do you think?"

"It's beautiful."

"You picked a great color," the young man said. "You can never go wrong with white. It makes a house look bigger, neater, and cleaner. Plus your dark green shutters add character to the home."

She tried to listen as he continued to talk. Obviously, he was older than she thought.

"And if you ever get tired of the dark green, you can always have them painted; black and dark blue are popular shutter colors right now. But the green definitely looks good on your house, with all the flowers and plants and stuff."

The more he talked, the more tickled Lottie got. She bent over at her waist and rested her hands on her knees. *He probably thinks I'm having a heart attack.* She let out an unmistakable giggle. Just as he was bending over to look at her face, she shot straight up. A deep laugh rushed from Lottie's throat, startling the young man. "Glory hallelujah!" She clapped her hands together so loud it sounded like the Church of God had joined in.

"I take it you're happy with the job." He fanned his face with the clip board.

"I'm beyond happy. I feel like I've had a glimpse of heaven and seen my mansion." She looked into his big blue eyes. "Have you got a mansion waiting for you, son?"

The young man blinked; he didn't know exactly what she was talking about and was afraid to ask. "I don't know if I do or not, Mrs. Johnson."

"Well, I promise you the Lord Jesus has a special one built just for you, but you can't have it unless you know the builder. Do you know Jesus like you know your mama and your daddy?"

"No, ma'am, I don't. Am I suppose to know him that good?"

"Yes, sir. That's the only way to know him—personally. It don't do no good to know about him, like knowing about Elvis. Why don't we pray and ask him to introduce himself?"

"Right here, in the yard?"

"Son, God don't have a problem with it if you don't."

He bowed his head as Lottie lifted hers toward heaven; her voice rising as it floated over the weathered fence and through the branches of thick oaks.

Lottie stepped onto the porch and smiled; her hands clasped in front of her. The kids stepped off the bus one by one. Had she known she was expected to give a guided tour, complete with planting, pruning, and fertilizing information, she probably would have spent the night by the commode, but since it all happened so quick, she did an outstanding job. She couldn't resist putting Rebecca on the spot at times, referring a curious boy's question to her instead. Lottie gave her a proud smile, quickly straightening her shoulders and giving her head a tilt upward just fast enough for Rebecca to respond with the same gesture. *That's my girl.*

Today Dovie informed me that Edgar made an appointment with a counselor at Alcoholics Anonymous. She said she didn't encourage him or discourage him. Poor Dovie. This has broken her heart. She loves Edgar like a son. So, we'll see what happens.

The church has been surprisingly supportive and understanding; no whispering about Edgar behind me in the pew and no unwanted telephone callers picking for information. The elders anointed Dovie with oil last Sunday night during the altar call. I sure am glad we have the church body.

Rebecca is dealing with it in her own way. Who am I to tell her she must forgive? She and Edgar usually talk a few minutes on Fridays before he goes to work, but she left my house early today. Maybe next Friday she'll be able to look him in the face. I haven't been able to yet. We'll soon see if Edgar has had enough of himself.

Jasmine

Chapter Ten

Rebecca thought about lunch at Lottie's all through Sunday school and preaching. She stepped through the front door and walked into the kitchen. Her mouth watered. The aroma of fried chicken clung to the inside of the house like a polyester dress to pantyhose. Fresh biscuits, snow white and soft to the touch, sat proudly on a blue plate on top of the stove while hot peppered gravy, the color of coffee with extra milk, thickened in the large frying pan.

Rebecca pulled her finger out of the mashed potatoes just as Lottie walked by.

"All I can say is your hands better be clean." She popped Rebecca on the backside.

"I told you to get out from over that food," Marie said.

"I'm starving to death, Mama. We've been out a lot longer than Miss Lottie. They don't have clocks at her church."

"Well, it's ready to eat now. Set the table and I'll fix the tea. I thought we were going to eat light today, Lottie. Did Fletcher's have their fryers on sale?"

"Sure did. You know I can't resist a good fried chicken. I ate a wing already."

"You must be starving, too." Rebecca folded the paper towels neatly before placing them beside each plate.

"Wait 'til I tell you about Bishop Clemmons' message. Lord have mercy, I never heard such in all my life. I was hanging on every word, writing as fast as I could. Between Brother Jones'

'Tell it now,' behind me and Dovie's, 'Thank ya, Sir,' beside me, it was all I could do to get it down. Ya'll go ahead and fix your plates. I'm going to get my notebook."

Rebecca waited until Lottie was down the hall. "Mama. We got to hear another sermon?"

Before Marie could answer yes, Lottie was back.

When everyone was seated around the table and the blessing said, Lottie proceeded to redeliver the morning message. "Brother Clemmons said our life experiences can be compared to visits to the hospital. The first room we come to is the waiting room. You know we all hate to wait, especially when we're trying to hear from God about something. Well, in the waiting room we wait; that's all we do. In our lifetime we make trip after trip there because it's in the waiting times that we're still and can hear from God."

Rebecca took a bite out of the chicken leg, then wiped the grease from her mouth.

"Sometimes we're placed in the examining room. Like when God starts putting his finger on areas in our life that are not right. The Holy Ghost examines our hearts, our insides. He said we're all gonna be in the examining room lots of times; sometimes the exams hurt and sometimes they don't."

Rebecca quickly swallowed her mouthful of warm, potatoes and gravy and raised her hand. "I think I know what the next room is."

"What?" Lottie asked.

"The restroom."

"Girl, I'm trying to preach here. No, the next room is the operating room. Once God has examined you and put his finger on the area in your life that needs to be removed or repaired, then he operates."

"Ouch!" Rebecca said, giggling.

"That's not how I'd describe it, would you, Marie?"

"No. It's more like wailing with screaming and kicking mixed in. You'll understand soon enough, Rebecca."

Lottie took a drink of her tea and continued. "Like the waiting room and the examining room, the operating room will be visited and revisited during a lifetime. But there is a difference. We have to give our okay before the surgery can take place. Just like when we have real surgery today, we have to sign our name in agreement."

Rebecca had never had surgery. She wondered what it would be like as she listened to Lottie continue.

"The last room we visit is the recovery room. It's in the recovery room that we mend and heal. Some of our safest times are here. We've been examined, poked, and prodded, cut on, and stitched up. Now we recover; safe under God's watchful eye." Lottie looked up and closed the notebook.

Marie broke the silence. "Well, I'll certainly remember that sermon."

"I'll remember it, too," Rebecca added. "Mama, since she just preached, do we have to go back to church tonight?"

Lottie slid her cool feet into the fuzzy slippers and tied the belt tight around her cotton robe. She carried a bowl of cornbread and milk into the living room and turned on the television. She had looked forward to tonight's episode of *The Carol Burnette Show* ever since she read in the *TV Guide* that Aretha Franklin would be the special guest. Harvey Korman and Tim Conway were two of her favorite comedians, too. Sometimes she laughed so hard she cried.

Carol had just finished answering questions when Lottie's phone rang. After five rings, uneasiness filled her stomach; ten rings brought on sweaty palms which gripped the blue velour arms of the recliner. After the fifteenth ring, she stomped to the kitchen, jerked the receiver off the hook and spoke fast through clinched teeth. "What? I'm trying to watch *The Carol Burnette Show*."

"Lottie, this is Dovie. I need you to come over to the house quick."

"What's wrong? Are you having a heart attack? Call 911."

"No, I'm not having a heart attack, it's heart ache and I need someone to talk to. You know Edgar's at work."

"Have you tried Odelia or Althea? What about Clovis or Leander?"

"I can't talk to them about my problems. You know how they gossip. Lord, the whole town would know all my business in the morning if I called one of them. You the only friend I trust with my secrets."

Lottie heard Dovie blow her nose in the background. She put her fingers on her temples and squeezed hard. "I'll be right over, Dovie." She hung up the phone hard and walked back into the living room. She turned off the television just as Carol introduced Aretha. Mumbling to herself, Lottie grabbed the flashlight from the top shelf in the closet.

She paused at her front door and said a quick prayer, asking the Lord to help her say the right words to Dovie. Then she poked her head outside to make sure there were no cars driving past. It was bad enough to be seen traipsing over to Dovie's house at nine-fifteen, much less wearing night clothes. Her steps were quick, like a cat running through damp grass: skipping, tiptoeing, and dodging. When she reached Dovie's front door, she pounded and shouted, "Open the door, Dovie, it's me."

Dovie's porch light glared into Lottie's eyes. She turned around again to see if any cars were coming. Just then, she heard the thud of Dovie's footsteps as they approached. "Who is it?"

"Dovie, open this door. You know who it is."

"I don't ever open my door unless I know the person on the other side. What's my favorite snack?"

"Anything sweet, now open this door before I kick it in!" Lottie fixed her glowering eyes on the front door.

"Oh, good, Lottie, it's only you. I was scared to death."

"Are you crazy? You just called me to come over. I was watching the *Carol Burnette Show*."

"Yeah, I was too. Aretha just finished. Lord, that woman can sing, can't she?"

Lottie walked through the front door, shaking her head. *I bet God's rolling over this one. Yeah, go ahead and laugh.* "You must be feeling better. Do you really need me over here?"

"Yes, I do. Come on in and sit down. I'll make us some hot chocolate. How about a piece of cake?"

"No cake, but the hot chocolate sounds good." Lottie sank deep into the brown and blue velvet couch. Three variegated afghans draped over the back formed a soft head rest and clashed hard with the other colors swirling around the room. Her eyes followed row after row of bric-a-brac, knickknacks, and whatnots arranged neatly on shelves housed in wooden cabinets. Dovie had at least one of every Avon bottle ever manufactured displayed proudly in a separate case. Her collection of salt and pepper shakers had their own living space between the collection of frogs and the collection of spoons. Lottie's head buzzed.

Dovie carried the hot chocolate on a silver tray.

A sting of conviction hit Lottie when she looked at Dovie's face and realized she was still crying. "What in the world has got you so upset? Did you get a bad report from the doctor?"

Dovie barely had enough time to put the tray down on the coffee table before she burst into uncontrollable sobs.

"Oh, help me Jesus. You got to calm down now, Dovie. I can't handle all this. If you got to cry, at least be quiet about it."

After a few minutes, Dovie was able to talk. "I guess you know me and Woody's been talking for about six months."

"Woody who?"

"Gist. You know, he was married to Promethia. She's been dead about three years now, and me and Woody's been talking on the phone. We've been out to eat ribs a time or two. Well, Leander called me tonight and told me that Odelia heard from Clovis that he's been sending flowers to women all over town. And that's not the worst part. Not only is he two-timing on me, but he ain't never sent me not the first flower." She started to cry again.

Lottie rubbed her forehead and then the back of her neck. Her eyes closed as she let out a deep sigh. *She'll feel better if I tell her. If I don't I'll be over here all night and I'm tired.* "All right. I know all about Woodward sending the flowers to ladies around town."

"You do? And you didn't bother to tell me? You had me going around town looking like a fool?"

"Dovie, don't blame that on me. Let me finish. Promethia died of cancer. Woodward decided one way he could help other cancer victims was to send flowers to help cheer them up. He was faithful to give Promethia flowers every week. He knew what good they did her and he wanted to help other people in the same situation."

"Are you saying that all those women he sent flowers to have cancer?"

"No, not all of them. But I do know that two of them do."

"What about all the rest of them? Leander said that Odelia said that Clovis said there's ten or eleven women."

"There are not! There are only six. One lady lost her grandson two weeks ago and another lady had a birthday last month."

"Well, I just had a birthday four months ago and he never sent me any flowers."

"Dovie, he sent birthday flowers to Ma Wannamaker. She's 93-years-old. Is she really competition?"

They looked at each other without speaking.

Dovie dabbed her eyes again and said in a weepy voice, "Well, what about all them flowers delivered to the bank on Friday? I was in there and saw Marie give vases to Ida Belle Tate and Mrs. Nash. Did Woody send them?"

"No. Ida Belle got flowers from her parents because of her promotion, and Mrs. Nash got flowers from her husband for their thirtieth wedding anniversary."

Dovie was hot on her trail like a prize-winning coon dog. Lottie grabbed the throw pillow beside her and held on.

Dovie coughed into the tissue, then wiped her dry eyes. "What about Nadine Nelson? The whole town knows she's got a married man for a boyfriend. Who sent her flowers Tuesday? Odelia saw her walking out of the plant with them after shift change."

"I can't say who sent them. That ain't none of my business."

"None of that other was your business either, but you knew all about it." Dovie jumped up from the couch and started tapping her right foot against the floor. Her lips shrank to form a tight grip around her teeth. "What's going on here, Lottie? You've scolded me and chewed me out before about gossiping, and I repented and everything. Now look at you; you know all about Mt. Brayden. How come?"

Lottie bolted off the couch. "Listen here, Dovie Williams, you called me over here because you needed somebody to talk to. Now that you feeling better you want to get all up in my face and-all-and-everthang. Well, I don't have to explain nothing to you. I'm leaving."

"No you ain't. You gonna sit back down and tell me all about this little adventure. I done been knowing you too many years. You ain't got a friendly, sociable bone in your body and now all of a sudden you Dear Billy Graham Abby." Dovie stood with her fists lost in her hips, her face within two inches of Lottie's.

Both women breathed hard.

Lottie had a non-spiritual vision of Dovie picking her up and throwing her on the floor. She sat down.

"All right, Dovie. I'm gonna tell you something that only a few people know. And after I tell you, I don't want you asking me nothing else about it. It's not my place to be telling all that I know, even though most of it is just plain old goodness and kindness." She proceeded to tell Dovie all about the flower pressing and the memory cards.

Dovie settled down when Lottie was finished and apologized for being so hostile. She said it was the pressure of thinking multiple women were sharing her man.

Lottie rolled her eyes. She wasn't happy about having to tell her about the memory cards. She knew Dovie would be picking for information every chance she got. "Now that my show's over, do you mind if I go home and go to bed?"

"No, go ahead. I do feel so much better now that I know the truth. And all this time I let myself get worked up over nothing. Woody is such a kind man. Oh! Valentines Day!" Dovie squealed. "I know he'll send me flowers then. Listen, you got to come over here on the fifteenth and tell me who got flowers and who didn't."

"Did you listen to what I just said? I'm not telling you anything else about the flowers. And don't you ever call me when Carol Burnette is on!"

Miss Lottie made the suggestion after Rebecca brought home the assignment in conjunction with black history month.

"I've never heard of Madame C. J. Walker." Rebecca sat at Miss Lottie's kitchen table eating cookies. "What is she famous for?"

"She was the first black female millionaire, that's all. And she helped a lot of other black women make a decent living by using and selling her products."

"What products did she make?"

"That, my girl, you'll have to find out on your own. Shall we take a walk to the library?"

"Yes, ma'am. My report is due Friday. I need to get busy."

They trudged through mounds of golden yellow, brown, and russet leaves on the sidewalk. Rebecca kicked her feet, sending the colorful litter high into the air and stirring up rich odors like memories that only come around once a year.

"You know what I like best about this season?" Lottie asked.

"What?"

"I love the smell of fallen leaves. It reminds me of eating crisp apples when I was younger."

"You can't eat apples anymore, though." Rebecca said, feeling sorry for her.

"No, I can't. I haven't bit into a fresh apple in so long I hardly remember what they taste like."

Rebecca shuffled her feet through the leaves. "You know, if you got dentures, you'd be able to eat apples and all kinds of good stuff."

Miss Lottie stopped walking and turned around, staring in her direction.

"Is something wrong?" Rebecca asked.

Lottie paused. "Remember when you told me about Patricia and Mary always wearing silky ribbons in their hair and how you didn't feel pretty enough to fix up your hair like that?"

"Yes, ma'am."

"Well, I've thought about dentures a time or two, but I never felt—" Lottie paused to breathe in the crisp October air. "I guess in the back of my mind I never felt like I was worthy enough to have dentures."

"Miss Lottie, that is a lie straight from hell. The devil don't ever want us to know how special we are. If anybody deserves to have dentures, it's you. You're the head and not the tail. You're blessed coming and going. Remember? We done been through this."

"Lord have mercy. You right. Yes, ma'am. You right. I guess I'll have to pay another visit to Mr. Radcliff."

Rebecca jumped up and down. "Does that mean you're going to get dentures?"

"I believe so. How is it you can make a simple statement and a light bulb turns on inside my head?"

Rebecca smiled and shrugged.

Rebecca stood before the class and gave her oral report on Madame C. J. Walker. She described the hair products Madame Walker created years before: shampoos, conditioners, lotions and curling irons. She kept everyone's attention, spoke clear and loud, and received the only A in the class.

She decided on the way home from school that she was ready to see Edgar. It had been three weeks since they'd talked. When she walked into Lottie's living room, there Edgar sat. His face was tense and his body rigid. Rebecca's fingers fumbled with the seams on the sides of her blue jeans. She'd just stepped into a serious discussion between Lottie and Edgar. She decided to get some Kool-Aid in the kitchen. After their voices quieted, Rebecca poured two more glasses and carried them into the living room. Evidently they had settled things; it was easier to breathe. "I thought you two could use some Kool-Aid."

"Thank you, Rebecca," Lottie said.

"Yeah, thanks," Edgar said without looking up.

Rebecca hoped Lottie would start on supper or go outside. She needed to tell Edgar she had forgiven him. Instead, the three of them talked about the heat and humidity.

A few minutes later, Lottie stood, rubbed her lower back, then jingled the ice cubes in her glass. "Well, I think it's time to start the meatloaf."

"I need to head back to the house, too."

"But you don't leave for work until after four." Rebecca's words rushed out. "Stay and we'll talk. Do you want to sit on the trampoline?"

Once outside, Edgar was the first to speak. "I've missed our visits, Rebecca."

"I have too. So many things have happened since—" She turned around and hoisted herself up on the side of the trampoline.

"Go ahead and finish. Since what?"

"Since you got drunk, humiliated us, and broke Dovie's heart."

Edgar smiled. "Don't hold anything back now, just give it to me straight."

Once Rebecca realized he was joking with her, she laughed. "Guess what? I made the only A in the class on my oral report. And I might be getting an extra five dollars if I get all A's on my report card."

"Sounds like you've been working hard." Edgar rubbed his shoe across the grass. "The only thing I can tell you is that I haven't had a drink in three weeks—not since I got drunk, humiliated ya'll, and broke Dovie's heart."

"I know you're trying to make this less awkward, but that's really not funny."

"I know. I'm sorry. I'm ashamed of the things I've done. I know Dovie's forgiven me and Lottie is working on it. I hope you will be able to forgive me, too."

"I already have. I sat you down in a chair in front of me last night. Mama told me to do it that way, so I did. It worked. I told you that I understood you had troubles inside that were too big to handle, but I believed you and God—working together—could make everything right. Mama also reminded me to pray for you every day. She said leaving alcohol behind is not an easy thing to do."

The breeze rustled the few remaining leaves above them. Finally, he spoke. "Thank you for everything, especially for praying for me."

There were times when Lottie regretted never having learned how to drive. As she listened to the wind howling outside, her first thought was she should have taken Marie up on the offer for driving lessons. *Oh well, I need to keep these old bones moving.* She wrapped the black scarf tight around her neck. Familiar raw air reintroduced itself as they walked together down Kelly Street. She recognized the odorless waft of wintry air as it made its way around the back of her head and settled gently on her exposed cheeks and nose, like weightless calm. Instead of resenting winter's visits, Lottie decided to rest in them, knowing that soon enough spring would return.

She vowed to be kind and thoughtful as she pushed open the double doors of First Savings Bank. She quickly walked to the receptionist's desk and asked to speak to Mr. Radcliff.

After a few minutes, he stepped around the corner. "Good morning, Mrs. Johnson, what can I do for you?"

"I just stopped by to take care of a personal matter. How's that little girl of yours doing?"

"It's awfully nice of you to ask. Suzanne is wonderful. We don't know what we did without her. She's got a lot of hair and she's chubby. And we're finally able to get some sleep at night." He chuckled. "How did you know we had a little girl?"

"Rebecca and Mary are good friends. You know how young girls are, they tell you everything that's going on."

"Right. Uh, Mrs. Johnson, do you have a minute? I'd really like to talk to you about something."

"I sure do, just as long as you don't keep me too long. I have an appointment." They turned and stepped into his office. Lottie immediately noticed the dark bookshelves lined with books behind his desk and the gold-framed pictures of his family. The polished brass name plate sat in front of her as a reminder of where she was. She sat down in the leather chair.

"Mrs. Johnson, I realize you live a contented life at your home on Kelly Street, and I don't want to cause you any distress by bringing up this subject, but I'd really like for you to think about this." He appeared hopeful for a favorable response.

"Go ahead, I'm listening."

"Your property, as you know, is very much desired by the city but, and I emphasize this, you could profit enormously from the sale of it if you choose to do so. It seems to be a win-win situation."

Lottie thought about his words for a moment before she spoke. "What would Mt. Brayden build there if I sold it?"

"I'm sure some type of business or retail store; maybe a drug store. The need for new office space has been discussed as well."

"Well, I appreciate the offer. I've never considered selling before, and I'm not saying I'm considering it now, but I will think about it, Mr. Radcliff."

"That's good enough for me, Mrs. Johnson. Now, can I help you with anything out here?" He walked her into the lobby.

"No, thank you just the same. Have a nice day."

"You, too."

Standing before the teller, Lottie realized that her hands gripped her purse straps so tight, they were numb. She tucked the money deep inside her purse, then turned to leave, stopping briefly in the foyer to wrap the scarf around her neck. She breathed in deep and exhaled slowly. *Well, Lord, I did handle it pretty good. Did I really tell him I'd think about it?*

She marched down Main Street past Marie's shop. Her concentration turned from Mr. Radcliff to Dr. Satterfield. Her stomach fluttered. *Some things you just got to do. It'll be over with soon enough.* Lottie pushed open the door and walked up to the counter. "Mrs. Johnson," she told the receptionist seated behind the sliding glass window.

"Thank you, Mrs. Johnson. Please fill out the front of this form and bring it back to me when you're finished."

Lottie noticed her name tag and remembered the vase of yellow roses. *How sweet to get flowers on your anniversary.*

She couldn't be married but a couple of years; she looks so young! Lottie found a seat by the window and filled out the form. When she returned to the window she acted surprised to see the wedding ring on the young girl's hand. "Kerry, that's a beautiful wedding ring you have on. My goodness, you look too young to be married."

"I've been married for two years now. We just celebrated our anniversary in August." Her face beamed.

"Well, congratulations. Oh, Marie Mathis from Main Street Florist will be picking me up after everything is done. Will you call her?"

"Yes, ma'am, I sure will. Let me write that down."

Lottie returned to her seat and pulled out a small paperback from her purse. Losing herself in a good book was easy to do, normally, but today she was getting a new set of teeth. All morning long her tongue rubbed over the remaining few, memorizing their familiar place. Six teeth may not seem like much, but when they're all you have left, there's a strong attachment, almost a promise made as to their protection. Now the time had come to say good-bye to a part of her and meet, through blood and pain, strangers. Her small mouth was now expected to house a full set of dentures. Perfect dentures.

She contemplated the situation. Would that be like a grandmother parading around in hot pants? So what if Granny could fit into a size eight. Did the hot pants go with the rest of the package? Probably not, but it was too late now.

"Mrs. Johnson, we're ready for you to come on back," Kerry said.

Lottie shoved the unread paperback into her purse and got up slowly from the chair. Her feet were reluctant to move. "Let's go get them hot pants, Granny," she mumbled to herself.

After six weeks Lottie's mouth had healed. She was even able to eat some foods she hadn't been able to eat before. Sitting outside, bundled up in their thick coats and scarves, Lottie and Rebecca enjoyed their first crisp red apples—together.

Maybe I shouldn't write about it, but I'm going to anyway. I had never been with a man until the day me and Jerome got married. Mama tried to tell me about how our wedding night might be but she got embarrassed and I did, too. Anyway, the last thing she said was, "Lottie, honey, you'll do just fine." I guess if she'd told me the truth about how it would be, I'd have been too scared to crawl in that big old bed.

Me and Jerome only had about four and a half years together as man and wife. I never had much time to learn about the secret things that go on in the marriage bed, in the dark, still night. Now I've had all these years to know what I've missed. Jerome would put his left arm around my waist and his right arm around my neck. He'd squeeze me so tight my breasts would sting. I'd get mad and push him away. Say something like stop that carrying on. If I knew I only had four and a half years with him, I would of—well, I wish I'd known so I could have memorized all the things he did to me. And I never would have pushed him away.

Chapter Eleven

Edgar had postponed the event twice already. Now that Thanksgiving was just around the corner he knew his sponsor, Will Hopkins, would insist that he visit the old home place soon.

"Even though the holidays can be extra hard for recovering alcoholics, I think you're ready to meet the challenge. Facing your fears during this time of year could catapult you into advanced recovery," Will said to Edgar while the rest of the group took a break.

"But I don't have any ugly holiday memories, so why is it so important that I visit the place now?"

"It was important that you do it three months ago, but since you put if off so many times, I decided that the Thanksgiving holidays would be your launching pad. I know you can do this, Edgar. Now's the time to confront your past. Besides, you'll have a couple of days off work to recuperate."

"Is that supposed to make me feel better?"

"You may not see it as a plus now, but next week you will. What about Friday, the day after Thanksgiving?"

Edgar heard the others returning to the room. Their voices were muffled, unlike earlier when they stood behind the podium and revealed private information that caused Edgar to cross and uncross his legs every minute or so and move from side to side in his chair as he clasped and unclasped his hands. He was ready to leave. "Next Friday is fine. I'll take a notebook and cover my story like a professional reporter. Or should I use a tape recorder?"

"I know you're being sarcastic but neither one is a bad idea. Listen, has it ever occurred to you that since you don't remember any ugly holiday memories that maybe there were only good ones?"

"I know there were only good ones. I just don't see why it's so important to remember them."

"Well, what memories do you want to remember if not the good ones?"

Edgar didn't answer. Someone behind him coughed. He walked back to his seat, crossed his arms over his chest and chewed on his lower lip. *Happy Holidays.*

Dovie cooked so much food Thanksgiving day, Edgar had to set up two extra card tables to hold everything. He'd met both of Dovie's daughters, Estelle and her family, and Stella and her bunch. The rest of the brood he didn't know a thing about; after ten minutes with them he wanted to keep it that way. He excused himself and walked next door to Lottie's.

Lottie crossed her arms and shook her head. "I told you the rest of Dovie's family was weird. I bet somebody brought potato chips didn't they? And sauerkraut and weenies?"

"Yep. How many times have you been over there for Thanksgiving?"

"Only once, but things like that you don't forget. What about Dovie's sister, Eunice? She got there yet?"

"She was the first one through the door."

Lottie laughed. "Let me guess. She brought her famous prune and fig pie with bananas on top."

"You've had more than one Thanksgiving over there."

"No, I have not. Believe me, if you'd heard Eunice's breakdown of why the pie's ingredients were essential to good digestion—plus having to choke down a thick slice—the nightmare would be etched in your intestines, too."

Edgar stared up at the ceiling. "What am I supposed to do, now? Dovie's done told all of them how much I love to eat."

"That's your problem, Edgar. I'm going to join Marie and Rebecca for tender turkey breast, cornbread dressing, sweet potato soufflé, green beans, fat back, rolls, and fresh cranberry sauce. Oh, I left out the pumpkin and pecan pies."

"Well, I'll just stay over here and watch television or something. You got bologna and cheese in there, don't you?"

"Edgar, you're just fooling yourself. That crowd don't take no for an answer. They'll be here in ten minutes if you ain't got back over there. And I guess you done figured out that Stella is loose as a goose."

"The first thing her daughter said to me was, 'My mama ain't got no husband and I ain't got no daddy.'"

"You better start asking the Lord for a double portion before you step foot back in that house."

"You mean take two portions of all that food?"

"Lord have mercy, Edgar! Get in the Word before you carried off to an idolatrous land or turned into a pillar of salt."

"Speak English, Lottie, and hurry up!" He rushed to the window and looked out. "They'll be over here any minute."

"Well, I'm not proud of what I'm about to tell you, but it works. I tried it a few years ago when Dovie had her family reunion."

"You went?"

"I had to! She called me every day for a month; she came over a dozen times. I even got four postcards in the mail. I think their family tree goes straight up. But, here's what you do. First, fill up your plate with Dovie's food and thank God for each delicious bite. Then make a big deal about going back for seconds, which will be what everybody else cooked. Then yell loud and hold the side of your face like you just bit a big hunk out of your cheek. That's what I did, and nobody bothered me anymore about eating."

Edgar scratched his head. "What if they remember you doing it?"

"Who cares? Tell them the Dewberry's have oversized teeth and small mouths."

"Dovie will get a big laugh out of that one."

Lottie crossed her arms. "Let her laugh."

A heavy knock rattled the front door. Lottie patted Edgar's shoulder, walked to the door, and opened it. Edgar could see Stella's hair from where he stood. It was stacked so high she could have been Diana Ross and all the Supremes. Her artificial eyelashes were in front of him before the rest of her body was. Then came the rest of her body: multiple generous endowments popped out of her low-necked blouse, swallowed up her too-tight belt, and bulged out the back of her seam-stretched skirt. Her expanse left a lasting impression. She sashayed in front of the mirror on the wall beside Edgar, turned around, cocked one hip to the side, then rested her open hand on top of it. Edgar imagined other things resting on top of that hip: a plate, a book, a map of Tennessee.

"You coming back, Eddie?"

Lottie held up her hand. "Hold your horses, Stella. Edgar was just telling me about all the wonderful food ya'll got stacked up over there."

Stella bounced her hip up and down three times. "I come from a long line of cooks. Cooking and happy-home-making are my greatest assets."

"I'm positive you got others, Stella," Lottie said, then smiled at Edgar. "Well, Eddie, I'm going to stroll over to Marie's for din-din."

Edgar stuttered before real words came out. "I'll take care of that problem shortly, Lottie. Let me go over and fix a plate first."

Lottie played along. "Okay. There's no need to hurry, though."

"Yeah, Eddie. It's Thanksgiving. You shouldn't work on holidays."

"It's an emergency. Lottie's water pipes are leaking and termites are eating her sub flooring as we speak."

"It can wait until you get back tonight. Go enjoy yourself." Lottie grinned.

"Let's go then. I want to get to know this mystery man who's staying with my mama." Stella turned and walked to the door.

"Very good, Eddie," Lottie whispered. "I hope my house is still standing when I get back."

"Why you got to go acting like that, Lottie? I'm scared of that woman. She's liable to—"

"Hurry up, Eddie," Stella shouted from the porch. "The food's getting cold."

"Coming."

Edgar still tasted the prune and fig pie. Lottie's plan had failed, which left him trapped at Dovie's like a fish in a fish hatchery. He rolled over and pulled the bedspread under his chin. Her laughter still rang in his ears. After everyone left Dovie's last night, he called Lottie. When she finally answered the phone, all he could hear were spurts of laughter.

"Am I ever going to hear the end of this?" he asked her.

"I didn't say a word."

"You didn't have to. I just called to let you know the bite-the-cheek act was a dud. After I did it Dovie leaned over and whispered in my ear, 'It won't work, Edgar.' All I could do was force feed myself and hope I could keep it all down." He knew it was funny but he refused to laugh along with Lottie. To reinforce his irritation, he hung up the phone without saying good-bye.

Edgar heard Dovie's feet clamor past the bathroom and stop at his door. She knocked softly. "Just a minute." Edgar jumped out of the bed and threw on his flannel robe. The floor was cold under his bare feet. "Come in."

"Good morning. You still stuffed from yesterday?"

Edgar saw mischief in her eyes. "No, not really. Eunice's prune and fig pie took care of that. If you have another family gathering, promise me one thing."

"What's that?"

"Promise me you'll be on my side."

Dovie laughed. She slapped her thigh which made a dull thud sound through her chenille robe. "Okay. How about you stick up three fingers, turn around once, and then pat your belly. That could mean I'm stuffed; don't force me to eat another bite. If you tap your finger on the left side of your head and scratch under your arm, that could mean I'm enjoying myself and everything is okay."

"I'll never remember any of that. Besides, if we create some sort of code, it needs to be discreet. I mean, your family's not the brightest around but even they would get suspicious with all those body motions going on."

"You're right. Especially the part about my family not being the brightest. That's all the more reason I thank God daily for my mind. It's sharp, quick, powerful, and quite complicated, really. Still waters run deep, you know."

"I really don't know. What exactly does that mean?"

She thought a minute. "Well, it means that deep-thinking people have a well of wisdom to draw from."

"I wonder why nobody ever said turbulent waters run deep?"

"Turbulent waters don't run deep. It's as simple as that. It's down in the deep, dark places that stillness is found. And in that stillness is where wisdom lives. I'm not bragging, but I can feel the weight of wisdom deep inside of me."

"Oh, I believe you. But if you were a short person, say five feet, you wouldn't be as wise as you are now because there wouldn't be any extra room for wisdom like you got now in them king size legs and them colossal feet."

Dovie laughed as she slapped Edgar on the arm. "Very funny. I thought you stumbled on something profound." She pulled the belt of her robe tighter. "What are you doing today since you're off work?"

He plopped down on the side of the bed. "Will wants me to visit our old house on Salters Creek Road."

Dovie stepped closer and rubbed his shoulder. "You can do it, Edgar. And I know you'll feel better."

"Yea. As soon as I take a shower I'm going over there. I just want to get it over with." He got up and started to make his bed.

"I'm going to cook breakfast. You want anything?" Dovie asked.

"Yeah, Kaopectate in a bowl."

Dovie's laugh followed her down the hall.

He drove Dovie's car slower than it had ever been driven. The Buick rounded the corner on Salters Creek Road, then slowly rolled into the dirt driveway. The post for the mailbox towered over brittle twigs and messy underbrush. The scent of dead leaves and frigid air seeped into the car. He didn't remember the driveway being so long.

The house came into view after Edgar crept past the old walnut tree. He used to have a tire swing he played on while his mama collected walnuts. She said one good thing about having dark skin was that no one knew when you had been messing with walnuts. The sound of crunching underneath the tires made him wonder if he had just ran over some.

A flicker of hope sparked inside him when he pulled directly in front of the house. Maybe it was locked or had a no trespassing sign posted. He closed his eyes and exhaled. *You can do this.*

The heavy car door creaked as he opened it slowly. *Just get it over with.* Edgar turned from the car and walked across the overgrown yard. He wondered if the daffodil bulbs they had planted still bloomed. He was relieved it wasn't spring.

The porch looked the same. The railings were without paint but they weren't rotten. He stepped up the uneven block steps and inched his way to the door. The cold knob twisted far to the right and the door opened without effort. *So much for the locked door.* Just as his right foot touched the dusty wooden floor a bolt of weighted emotions surged through him. They pressed in tight, forcing his lungs to gasp for air. His entire body trembled; tears stung his eyes.

He stood in what once was his living room. Remnants of cheap curtains fluttered as the wind blew through the broken window. A few holes in the wall were recognizable, especially the one beside the mantle which used to be white. One evening, several months after Jerome and Wy were killed, Edgar's daddy was drunk. He wanted to sit outside on the porch but it was freezing cold. His mama had tried to stop him already. "Daddy, you don't need to go outside. You know how sick you get in the wintertime." But alcohol made his daddy stronger and meaner. Edgar reached for the chair his daddy was carrying. He pulled the chair hard in one direction while his daddy yanked in the other. Just as his daddy let go of the chair, Edgar pulled with all his strength. He and the chair crashed into the wall, leaving a gaping hole and a lump the size of a lemon on Edgar's head.

Now Edgar stood in the very spot where he heard his mama's scream, and later, his daddy's apology.

He stumbled through the doorway and into the kitchen. The Formica counter, yellow with flecks of gold glitter, looked the same. There were more cigarette burns now. The counter was cold and gritty under his hand. The window above the sink was grimy and hard to see through. A faded blue curtain blocked the only ray of sun that could have invaded the room if the glass was not sooty and stained. His mama used to stand on the brown kitchen chair, arms stretched out over the sink, one hand resting on the side of the cabinet while the other wiped the glass until the only way you could tell there was a window there at all was by the wooden panes, unpainted, but straight and clean.

The worn spot on the floor in front of the sink was shaped like an oval wooden dough bowl, dark brown and smooth. Any flooring that used to be there was gone, removed and forgotten under tired, shuffling feet. Old newspapers and beer cans littered the floor of the kitchen and the entryway into the first bedroom; his old bedroom. He forced himself to continue moving.

The walls were still the same bright blue. Above his head hung the same antique brass light fixture that was supposed to hold three light bulbs but only ever held one. An abandoned wasp nest clung to the corner of the yellowed ceiling. He walked by the window where, an autographed picture of Nat King Cole used to hang. He opened the closet door and looked for her name. There it was. *Marlene.* And the words underneath her name. *I love Marlene.*

Edgar didn't remember feeling so strongly about her, but evidently he did.

He stepped out of his old bedroom and across the hall to what used to be his parents' room. He had rarely been in it. The door was always closed. Most nights he could see pale light escaping from underneath the doorway, and sometimes he could hear his mama and daddy talking softly. Any traces of life were long gone. The room was littered, dark and cold.

Edgar hesitated at the back door before he stepped onto the porch. The dank odor filled his nostrils before he had time to breath through his mouth. *Now I'll never get that smell out of my nose.* He waved his hand in front of his face in hopes of fanning fresh air his way. He turned to the right and the sight of the old barn struck him full force, like a boxing glove thrust in his stomach. His knees melted. Quickly, he gripped the hand rail beside the back steps. The cushioned layers of leaves crackled and crunched beneath his shoes. He walked slowly toward the barn door.

The weathered beam was heavy and hard to lift. Angled shafts of light illuminated the inside of the barn like searchlights, revealing and silent. One beam of light shown directly on the old worktable where he and his daddy used to piddle. Edgar swallowed hard. He stood where he had stood years before, hammering nails into a pretend project. He heard the pounding of the hammer's steel head against the crooked nail and beaten wood.

He dropped to the ground and closed his eyes.

The plowman forged ahead, relentless and determined. Old and new blood filled the trenches as the blade dug deeper. The old carried away useless debris while the new brought good seed that took root and lived. Uprooted pain withered and dried up in the warm November sun.

Lottie finished her conversation with Dovie and hung up the phone. She pressed the back of her hand against her lower back, returned to the window, and pulled back the curtain. Edgar's visit to his old home place was a major step, and Lottie spent the morning pacing, planning, and praying.

She thought of her many visits to Salter's Creek Road. Her memories of her aunt Edith and uncle HK were pleasant. She would help aunt Edith outside planting bulbs, hanging clothes, plucking chickens, and beating rugs. Inside, she helped with canning vegetables, making pies, darning socks, and churning butter. Chores were never-ending; except they didn't feel like chores at aunt Edith's. And on special occasions when the chores were caught up, Lottie would try on dresses too big and makeup too dark. She would pretend to be a star and sashay across the kitchen with different hats on: feathered, pearled and netted in grey, pink and white. Lottie learned early on that red was not a color to be worn by a godly woman.

Since Edgar wasn't born until years later, aunt Edith and uncle HK treated Lottie like their own child. She often spent the night with them.

Lottie leaned closer to the window and shielded her eyes from the sun. Still no sign of him. She sat back down on the couch.

Her memories of uncle HK were fewer but still sweet and vivid. He would take her with him down to the fishing hole behind the barn. The cane pole he made for her was too long, but Lottie insisted that he not make it shorter. She wanted the stinking fish as far away from her as possible once she caught it.

It was uncle HK who contributed more than anyone else to the cavities Lottie developed. They would ride to the Goodie Shop where Lottie would fill a small brown paper sack with Tootsie Rolls, Mary Janes, Chic-o-sticks, and bubble gum. Sometimes uncle HK would go to the barber shop and let Lottie sit in a tall chair and eat everything in the bag. She thought he let her eat it all because he understood how hard it was for a child to resist candy; the truth was he would get fussed at if aunt Edith knew he had bought her all that candy in the first place.

Lottie pushed herself up from the side of the couch. *Why don't I just leave the curtains open?* Finally, she saw Dovie's car creeping down the street. She strained to see Edgar's face as he passed by the house and slowly turned into Dovie's driveway. She let the curtain fall and jetted across the hall into her bedroom and close to the window. She could smell the Windex on the clean window panes. Edgar opened the car door with effort. He swung his feet to the side, then rested them on the gravel driveway. He used the car door to pull himself up and stand. His face was haggard.

Before he could close the car door, Dovie burst from the back door and pounded down the porch steps. On her tiptoes, Lottie could just barely see them talking, but she strained, without success, to hear what they were saying. Then Dovie smiled big and threw her husky arms around Edgar's neck.

Lottie let the curtain fall and thanked God for what had happened; whatever it was.

Lavender

Chapter Twelve

Lottie's Christmas season began like it had for years gone by: small artificial tree on the coffee table with a white piece of cloth wrapped around the stand; glittered bells attached to the front door; Nat King Cole's voice meandering effortlessly up, over, and around; and jeweled fruit cake batter heaped in greased black pans ready for the oven. *This is Christmas to me*. Lottie opened the oven door and breathed in the hot, sweet aroma.

Christmas should be this simple everywhere, or at least next door. Snapshots flashed before her: ladders, faded plastic figures, signs hammered into the ground, a manger, wreaths, candy canes, banners, and bows. And lights! Every year objects, whether alive or inanimate, were covered, smothered, and draped with lights. Lottie tin-foiled her bedroom window so she could continue to sleep nights from the day after Thanksgiving until January the tenth. *At least she turns that chipmunk record off at ten*.

Lottie dried the measuring cups and bowls, then put them away. She heard the repeated thud of a hammer. *Evidently Edgar failed to talk some sense into her*. She stepped onto the back porch, clutching her thick robe tight around her neck. The air was arctic. She could see Edgar on top of Dovie's house. He hoisted the dark complected Santa on top of the chimney, then strapped something around him to keep him in place.

Lottie surveyed the yard and shook her head. Although Dovie chose to call it "seasonal yard art," Lottie knew it was nothing more than an awful mess.

She walked back into the house and called Dovie on the telephone, something she rarely did. "Well, I see we gonna have another Christmas like last year with traffic backed up along the street, kids hanging out the car windows bellowing Christmas carols, your yard shining brighter than a car dealer's lot, and the Chipmunks squawking until ten."

"I know it's a wild guess but is that you, Lottie?"

"Dovie, why not tone it down this year? Make a change. You might like it. It'd be a lot less work."

"What I do, I do for others. It makes people smile and remember Christmases long past. What's wrong with that?"

Lottie hesitated. "There's nothing wrong with that, but every Christmas I get tired of living beside the fair. Why not hire people and set up booths around the yard, too? They could pull the children out of their cars and let them throw darts at red and green balloons or toss little wreaths around the necks of Pepsi bottles."

"Why don't you go serve at the soup kitchen or volunteer as a candy striper at General? Just when I thought you couldn't get no more hateful…"

Lottie heard Dovie's voice fade as she pulled the phone away from her ear and hung up.

At that moment, Lottie decided to spend Christmas away from Mt. Brayden. She waited until Edgar finished illuminating and decking before she asked him to come over.

"I'm so sorc I can barely move," he said. "Dovie's had me decorating every day this week. Starting tomorrow night she wants me to wear the Santa suit and sit on the front porch waving, tossing candy to the kids, and ho-ho-hoeing."

"If I was you, I'd be mo-mo-moving. She'll push you over the edge. You realize that, don't you, Edgar? You'll lose your mind."

"Well, I wouldn't go that far, Lottie. I'm just tired of all this decorating."

"Come sit down at the table and have a piece of fruit cake. I just made it." She walked to the cabinet beside the sink, opened the door, and took out two saucers and two glasses. "You deserve a break after all that mess. You know Dovie's obsessive compulsive, don't you?"

"Say what?"

"She's obsessive compulsive. I asked the receptionist at the mental health clinic what could make a person act the way 'my friend' acts. She told me 'my friend' sounded like a disordered obsessive compulsionist."

"I think you like to say big words."

She poured his milk and then slapped him on the shoulder. "I called you over here for a specific reason, so listen up. And don't drop any crumbs on the floor; I swept and mopped already."

Edgar smelled the slice of cake and took a big bite.

"I've decided to go see Uncle Hiram for Christmas."

A piece of candied cherry discharged from his mouth like a slug from a twelve gauge. "You talking about the great-uncle Hiram who lives in the old folks home, 97-years-old and nutty as this fruit cake?"

"Who else? How long has it been since we've seen him? Ten years? Fifteen?"

"What's it matter? He don't even know who he is much less who we are."

"You ort to be ashamed of yourself, Edgar. Uncle Hiram's the only relative we got left on the Dewberry side. The least we could do is visit him during the holidays...spread a little Christmas cheer."

"I see your mouth moving but that don't sound like you talking. What's your real reason for leaving?"

She sighed, relaxed her shoulders, and let her head fall back. "Dovie's loony, and she's sucking me into her whirling-swirling-winter-wonderland. I might as well be living next door to Zsa Zsa Gabor."

"That bad, huh?"

"That bad. You want to go with me?"

"I don't think so, Lottie."

"You know Estelle and Stella will stay over there with Dovie until January the first."

"January the first?"

"At least. Happy New Year."

Edgar burped into his paper towel. "I feel sick."

"Well, it's not because of my fruit cake. Your subconscious is being harshly awakened by a bad dream: Stella, stacked hair and layered backside, New Year's Eve kiss. Who knows, you could get tangled up in the moment and agree to marriage."

"Count me in. Make reservations with Budget Inn, two double beds, non-smoking, first floor. When are we leaving?"

"A week from today. Trailways leaves at six o'clock, arrives in Chattanooga at one. Just in time for lunch."

Edgar stood and pushed the chair back with his leg. "Thanks for the cake," he said as he walked to the door. "Are you even sure uncle Hiram's still alive?"

"No. If he ain't we'll sing carols over his grave."

"Either way we'll escape here alive," Edgar said.

"That's the way I see it."

The next day Edgar wrapped lights around the porch columns, windows, steps, and bushes. From what he could see, nothing was left unwrapped; except for the car.

"Hey, Edgar. Still decorating?" Rebecca asked.

"Of course."

She stepped up the walkway and over to where he was squatted. "Miss Lottie told Mama ya'll are going away for Christmas this year."

"Sure are. We're going to Chattanooga to see our uncle Hiram."

"Me and Mama are going to Atlanta to see Mama's best friend, Delta. We won't be around either."

"Well, good. Neither one of us has to feel bad about leaving the other behind."

She smiled. "Yea, I know."

"When are ya'll leaving?"

"Saturday. Same day as ya'll."

"I can't believe we're all going away for Christmas this year. Well, all except Dovie," Edgar said.

"That's okay, though. Her daughters and their families always come and stay with her until, like, way into the new year."

"So I heard."

"Do you think she'll mind? All of us being gone?"

"I'll let you know. I was going to tell her after we eat."

"Well, I'm going to Mary's. Let me know what she says." Rebecca turned and walked toward the sidewalk. "See ya."

After dinner Edgar washed and dried the dishes. He decided to let Dovie relax awhile before he told her about the trip. During dinner he imagined her screaming and crying and throwing red glass ornaments at him. What if she asked to go with them? He laughed out loud at the thought.

He tiptoed into the living room where Dovie reclined. Her feet were up, arms out, mouth open, and eyes shut. The Dallas Cowboys were playing the Washington Redskins in five minutes. He turned on the television, plopped down on the couch, and closed his eyes for just a second.

"Edgar, the game's over." Dovie leaned over the couch and poked him on the shoulder.

"What? Over? I just turned it on."

"You were out like Joe Frazier, snoring and everything."

He rubbed his eyes and sat up. He needed a glass of tea.

"This is gonna be the best Christmas ever. I got more of the yard lit up than I've ever had; Stella and Estelle will be staying with me until January the tenth; and the *Farmer's Almanac* is calling for a white Christmas. I just can't wait!"

"How about a glass of tea, Dovie?" Edgar asked.

"Sounds good. Maybe I'll have some more of that blackberry cobbler, too."

"Don't get up. I'll get it." A few minutes later he returned with tea, cobbler, spoons, and napkins. "Here you are, Madame."

"Edgar, you are truly the son I never had. You so swe-e-e-t."

He handed her the dish of cobbler. The couch felt spongier than usual as he sank low and closer to the springs.

"Have I asked you about being Santa Claus on Christmas? You know, put the gifts and toys out after the kids go to sleep?" Dovie took a bite of cobbler.

"No, you didn't. But listen, Dovie, I have something to tell you that I just found out yesterday and it's about Christmas."

"You don't want to sing carols on the sidewalk in the Santa suit?"

"No, I don't want to do that either, but that's not what I need to talk with you about."

"Let's have it then. I'm a big girl." Dovie smiled.

"When I was over at Lottie's yesterday, she sort of casually mentioned that she would like to see our uncle Hiram in Tennessee over the holidays."

"I remember Hiram. He's crazy."

"Well, I prefer the word senile, but anyway, Lottie asked if I'd like to ride with her and, you know, get away for a few days; see the country through a dirty Trailways window." He let out a partial laugh followed by a gulp of tea.

"That doesn't sound like a holiday. Sounds more like punishment."

"Lottie really feels like we need to see uncle Hiram one last time. You know he's 97-years-old."

"97 and crazy. He wouldn't know Lottie from Shelley Winters. Sounds like a wasted trip to me, but ya'll may be right. Hiram could be counting his days down as we speak."

"I know Stella will be disappointed that I won't be here. Would you explain the situation to her?"

"Sure I will. Don't worry about that. We'll have this place so full of people, food, and music, the windows will have to be cracked to release the pressure. You know Christmas is my most favorite time of the year."

"I gathered that."

She placed the saucer on the tray and walked over to the end table by the couch. "See this nativity set? This is the reason I love Christmas so much. All because of that little baby right there." Her fingers plucked Jesus from the wooden manger.

"That looks like an old set."

"It is. It belonged to my parents. I use it every year as a reminder to everyone who enters this home that if it wasn't for baby Jesus, there'd be no Christmas."

"That's nice. I remember we had Mary, Joseph, and baby Jesus, but that was all. You've even got the wise men, the animals, and the stable."

"But you know what? None of those other pieces matter anyway; just baby Jesus. All the rest are…well, decoration. Like what I got outside. I have the Christmas story on tape and it plays over and over every night. When the children lean out the windows to see all the lights and colors, they'll also hear some of the Christmas story; even if it's just a little portion."

Edgar put his arm around her shoulder and pulled her close. "Do you think that nativity set outside and the recording will make a difference in someone's life?"

"I know it will. God's Word won't return to him void. The Word of God floats out from that recorder, lingers beside the nativity set, rises above the trees, and wanders purposefully through the cold night air. I can see those precious words drip to the earth like drops of dew." She held up the tiny baby toward the light. "And it's all because of God's little baby."

"Just think, Miss Lottie, this time tomorrow me and Mama will be on our way to Atlanta and you and Edgar will be on your way to Chattanooga."

"I know it. The last few days sure flew by. Stand back now, while I open the door." Lottie reached in the hot oven and pulled out a thick pan of sugar cookies.

"They look so good I could eat them right now," Rebecca said.

"Oh, no you don't. These have to be decorated and sealed up. Some are for you and your mama to take to Atlanta and some are for Dovie and her house full of family." Lottie paused, her eyebrows furrowed. "Not that she needs anything else to eat over there."

"Edgar told me it took him thirty minutes to carry in all the groceries the other day, and almost an hour to put everything up," Rebecca said.

"I know. Why Dovie thinks she's got to go all out at Christmas is beyond me."

"But she does make the season more fun. I'm going over there later to make a gingerbread house with her."

"You are?"

"Yeah. She said she would have invited you to help but your hands aren't as steady as hers and she was afraid you'd mess up the decorating."

Lottie shook her head. "It just so happens I'm the one who got Dovie started making them gingerbread houses in the first place. About eight or ten years ago she was laid up over there with the gout. She couldn't do nothing but lay in the bed, so I suggested we make gingerbread houses; I'd bake them and she'd help decorate."

"She didn't tell me that."

"That old gingerbread-house-idea-stealer. I ort to go over there and—"

The ring of the telephone interrupted her ranting.

"Hello." Lottie paused. "You just the lowdown person I wanted to talk to. What are you doing telling Rebecca I can't decorate a gingerbread house?"

Rebecca strained to hear Dovie's reply.

"No, I wasn't drilling the child. She told me out of her own free will. And I couldn't care less about coming over there and helping, but the least you could have done was tell Rebecca the truth."

Miss Lottie's lips relaxed. Her hand dropped from her hip and her eyebrows lifted.

"Okay, okay. I guess everybody forgets now and then. Don't worry about it. I'm not gonna come over there and blow your gingerbread house down."

Rebecca giggled. Her hands loosened their grip on the sides of the kitchen table.

"Anyway, as soon as we finish with these cookies, I'll send her over. I've still got some packing to do." Lottie huffed and pulled out a chair. "No, I haven't had the television on. You know them eggheads never get the weather right. I ain't worrying about it. Let me go, Dovie. I got information overload. Okay, bye."

"What's wrong?"

"Not a thing. Dovie's getting herself all worked up because the weatherman says there's a winter storm headed our way out of Atlanta."

"Oh, no."

"Listen, tomorrow you'll be holding your breath crossing the Georgia state line, and I'll be holding mine crossing over into Tennessee. Dovie's a worry wart."

"I hope you're right," Rebecca said just before she turned to see her mama walk into the kitchen. "Mama, have you heard there's a bad storm coming?"

Lottie removed the last of the cooled cookies from the pan. "Dovie the weatherwoman's done got herself all worked up over nothing, I'm sure."

"That's what I came over here to tell you. I talked to Delta and she said it's already snowed two inches there and it's supposed to keep it up for the next twenty-four to thirty-six hours. We usually get our worst snow storms out of Atlanta."

Lottie's face paled. "You mean to tell me we gonna be snowed in here?"

"Looks like it. I know we won't be traveling to Georgia."

Rebecca stomped her foot. "Aw, Mama, I was looking forward to going."

"So was I, but we can't control the weather."

"Well, if this just don't beat all-and-everthang. I was ready to leave all the lights and fanfare behind. Now it looks like I'll be reliving the nightmares of Christmas past." Lottie reached to answer the phone. "Yeah. Yeah. Yeah. I know. Two inches. Well, I'm sorry Stella and Estelle and the gang won't be able to make it. We've got our own hardships over here. Marie and Rebecca can't go to Atlanta, and I'm sure Trailways won't be hauling nobody to Chattanooga." Lottie lowered the phone and rolled her eyes.

Lottie's shoulders slumped, her jaws clinched, and her head dropped in reluctant surrender. She mumbled okay and hung up the phone.

Marie pulled out a chair and sat down. Rebecca watched in silence. The red and green frosting had dried around the sides of the bowls. Suddenly, nothing on the table looked festive anymore.

"Dovie said to tell ya'll we all invited to spend Christmas Eve and Christmas Day at her house."

Rebecca jumped out of her chair and clapped her hands together. "Goodie!"

"Yeah." Lottie sighed, "Goodie, goodie, gumdrops."

Marie laughed and patted Lottie on the arm. "Come on, Lottie. It'll be fun."

"That's your opinion. I'd rather have a gynecological exam. The power will probably go out which means no heat. We won't have any water because we're on a well and, to top it all off, Dovie will rise to the occasion and be convinced she's been pre-ordained to entertain us with merriment and Christmas cheer. She'll take up the mantle of Esther and flit from kitchen to living room heralding, 'God hath prepared me for such a time as this.'"

Rebecca brushed her bangs to the side. "Man, Miss Lottie, you could have been a preacher."

The snow storm arrived earlier than expected. Lottie had just enough time to buy the last loaf of bread at Fletcher's and fill milk jugs with water in case the power did go off.

"Be careful on this snow. That's all we need is a broken ankle on top of all this," Marie said to Lottie as they walked arm in arm. "I can't believe you walked to my house in this mess by yourself."

"Well, the phones are out. How are we suppose to keep in touch? Mail a Christmas card? Plus, I wasn't about to go over to Dovie's without ya'll no way."

"Are you scared?"

"You doggone straight. And I'm aggravated and I'm mad as fire. I'm headed straight to prison."

"Just because we're spending Christmas Eve and Christmas Day with Dovie?" Rebecca asked.

"When you say it like that it don't sound so bad, but the reality of all this is once Dovie gets us locked up over there, we can't escape. She's gonna have a Fleece Noveltyda whether we like it or not."

Rebecca and Marie laughed out loud.

"Go ahead. Laugh, laugh, laugh. You'll see. We already been duped into spending Christmas Eve night over there. When all the snow hit the fan, we were only gonna go over for a few hours Christmas Eve and half the day on Christmas."

Marie pulled Lottie closer to her. "Try to remember that she's used to having her family with her every Christmas."

"She'd be lost if we didn't agree to spend the holidays with her," Rebecca added.

"I know all that, but I still can't look forward to incarceration."

"You could have told her you weren't coming," Rebecca said.

Lottie turned around and cut her eyes at Rebecca. "You got a lot to learn, kid. Have you ever known Dovie to take no for an answer? She'd be over at my house with the National Guard; I'd be hauled out like a roll of carpet. I just hope she'll leave me alone, let me rest in a quiet place with my wordsearch."

"That'll never happen," Marie said. They stepped over an iced section of uneven sidewalk.

"I tell you right now what I'm not doing. I'm not doing that Twelve Days of Christmas song with all them hand signals and-all-and-everthang. She tried to spring that on me the year of the gout. I felt sorry for her and all. That's when I went over and showed her how to make them gingerbread houses. Well, when I stopped by to see how she was Christmas Day, Estelle and Stella dragged me into the living room to help them sing "The Twelve Days of Christmas". I remember it vividly as my twelve minutes in hell."

Rebecca gasped. "Miss Lottie!"

"Sorry. I forgot you were back there." They stopped in front of Lottie's house.

Marie asked, "Do you have anything to take over: pajamas, records, games?"

"Very funny. I don't consider this a night with the girls and a cousin; I consider it a night in—"

"Don't even say it," Marie said.

"I do need to go inside and get my pillow and blanket. I already took my Christmas cookies and cider over," Lottie said.

"We'll watch the twinkling lights in Dovie's yard and listen to Bing tell the Christmas story. But hurry, my feet are frozen," Marie said.

Moments later, Lottie inched her way down the porch steps with her left arm clutching the pillow and blanket and her right gloved hand gripping the icy rail. "Okay, let's get this over with."

Edgar met them at the door with a cup of hot chocolate in his hand and a Santa hat on his head. "Welcome, weary travelers. Cometh thou in from the cold."

"And so the sentence begins." Lottie closed her eyes as she stepped through the door.

"You can put your pillow and blanket on my bed, Scrooge," Edgar said.

"She's still hacked about going to prison," Rebecca whispered.

"I'm sure with a little time, good food, and Dovie's holiday pressure, she'll come around to our way of thinking."

Lottie returned to the living room and looked around. "Edgar, where's the fake white tree and the rotating color wheel? I was so excited about seeing it again; so life-like."

"Dovie put it on the back porch so the back yard wouldn't feel left out."

"Where is Dovie, anyway? I don't hear her big—"

"Here I am, surrogate family."

Lottie eyes followed the shimmering red silk muumuu Dovie wore as it glided across the room.

"You look beautiful, Dovie."

"Thank you, Marie. I made it myself. I was going to sew little bells along the bottom but, less is more, you know."

Marie looked around the living room. "And the house is decorated so nicely. Where do you want me to put the sandwiches?" She followed Dovie into the kitchen. "It looks like you've got enough food here to feed the whole town."

"Well, I thought I'd have my family here, and you know there's fifty-two of us once you count the third and fourth cousins. I guess the Lord had other plans for our holiday."

"It was so good of you to invite us all over. It would have been lonely, just me and Rebecca at the house."

"I know. I'd go crazy if I'd had to be here all alone."

Lottie, Edgar, and Rebecca stood in the doorway of the kitchen.

"Ya'll want something to do?" Dovie asked.

They answered yes in unison.

"Edgar, you carry the punch bowl into the dining room and put it on the buffet. Rebecca, come get the cheese tray and crackers. Lottie, since you love my lemon bars, you can carry them. And if you'll carry the dip and chips, Marie, I'll carry the meatballs."

After four trips each, the dining room table and two fold-out tables were full. Lottie counted three kinds of dips; four kinds of sandwiches. There were cookies, cakes, pies, chips, a platter of chicken wings, ham biscuits, divinity, peanut brittle and mixed nuts. Four jugs of tea, Pepsis, and coffee sat on the kitchen counter while the punch, dark red with lime sherbet floating on top like icebergs in the Atlantic, sat on the buffet looking too pretty to drink.

Lottie stood in the living room gazing at the mother lode. "Edgar, all the preachers in Greenville and Spartanburg county, white and black, couldn't eat all this food. I sure hope she don't expect us to."

"It would be physically impossible for the five of us to eat it all."

"I bet Estelle and Stella could, just the two of them."

"I know that's right. You better hush, now. Don't let Dovie hear you," Edgar whispered.

Dovie walked into the dining room. "If you all will come on into the living room, we'll thank the Lord for his blessings." When everyone joined hands, Dovie began to pray. "We come to you, Father, with thanksgiving and praise in our hearts. For another day of good health, we say thank you; for another day of prosperity, we say thank you. Lord, for my precious friends I sincerely say thank you." She squeezed Lottie's hand. "Be with our loved ones who could not join us on this the eve of your birth. Comfort their hearts and ours as we are separated. Please bless this good food and allow us all, especially Lottie, to have fun and get loose. In the precious name of Jesus I pray. Amen."

Two hours later only a small dent was made in the food. What didn't have to be refrigerated was wrapped up and left where it was. What wouldn't fit in the refrigerator was taken to the front porch and placed on the porch swing.

Dovie read the Christmas story from the book of Matthew. They watched television for an hour, then sang Christmas carols around the piano. At nine-thirty Lottie tried to escape into Edgar's room but Dovie insisted the party had just begun. They played Rummy, Sorry, Monopoly, and Poker (which did not include placing bets with real money; red and green mints were used instead). At twelve forty-five Dovie had to help carry Rebecca and Lottie to bed. And so, Christmas Eve ended but there was still Christmas day.

Dovie knocked on the bedroom door. "Santa Claus left you something, Lottie."

"You can have it."

"Come on, now. It's six o'clock. We've done missed most of the morning. Let's sip coffee and talk around the table."

"No, Dovie."

"I got a key to this door. Don't make me go hunt it."

"I'll be out in a minute."

Edgar, Marie, Rebecca, and Lottie sat glassy-eyed around the sparkling tree listening to Dovie reminisce about her top-ten-most-memorable-Christmases-ever.

"And that's why Christmas 1953 is my all-time favorite. And now that I've shared my greatest Christmas memories, perhaps one of you would like to do so as well."

No one said a word.

Edgar's afro was flat on one side and perfectly round on the other. His mouth was partially open while he stared straight ahead like he was in a trance. Marie's eyes were weighed down with bulging luggage bags and if Rebecca had not been propped against Marie, she would have rolled quietly off the couch before Christmas 1922 had been shared.

Then Lottie spoke. "Look alive, ya'll. I got something to say." Edgar roused himself and rubbed his eyes. "This particular Christmas will stand out in my mind as the most memorable ever. And it's not because of all the food stacked up around here like boxes in a warehouse. And it's not because of the flashing lights, singing Santa, or the glittering tinsel. This will be my most memorable Christmas because it was spent in the company of friends. I have to admit, it would have been lonely at home by myself. That's all I got to say."

Edgar, Rebecca, and Marie sat dumbfounded.

Dovie's handclaps broke the silence. "How long you been going to Toastmasters?"

"Please, Dovie. I just said I'd remember this Christmas."

"That was a nice comment, though," Rebecca said as she batted her eyelids numerous times.

"Yeah, it was," Marie added.

Edgar laughed and clapped his hands. "I think it was repulsive and sappy and as soon as I get back to the dock, I'm gonna tell Clifton Jaw-Jacker what you said. It'll be all over Mt. Brayden in less than twenty-four hours."

Lottie jumped up and flung herself onto Edgar's back like a fly on a watermelon rind. She wrapped her long legs around his midsection; her arms wound tight around his head.

He couldn't see a thing.

"Get him, Miss Lottie, get him," Rebecca shouted.

"I'm getting out of the way in case they fall," Dovie said.

"Me, too," Marie said.

Rebecca pinched Edgar's back in different places and laughed each time he yelled. Lottie refused to let go even though Edgar stumbled around the living room and crashed into one of the card tables, sending sugar cookies and mixed nuts flying through the air.

Finally, Lottie loosened her grip. "Now, you gonna do any jaw jacking to Jaw-Jacker, big boy?" She waited. "I don't hear no answer."

His hands grasped Lottie's arms that wrapped around his head. "No, I ain't gonna do no talking. Now get off me!"

"Not until you apologize and call me what you used to call me when you were a little boy."

"Aw, come on, Lottie. Just get off me!"

"Say it."

"No."

"Say it."

Edgar whispered, "I'm sorry, Lovely Queen Lottie."

Chapter Thirteen

Winter passed. Buck, Steinbeck, and O'Conner took Lottie to places far and near. The library became her destination as she set out for walks, in sunshine or rain. She was growing and she needed to be fed.

Her memory cards were now alphabetically cataloged by the recipients' last names. So far, six full shoe boxes held Mt. Brayden's flower-giving history. Life's full gamut of important events were preserved there: life, death, sickness, proms, birthdays, weddings, anniversaries, and even repentance. Lottie began to see the commonness in the people of Mt. Brayden instead of their differences in relation to her. She chose to see what they were doing right instead of what they were doing wrong.

Edgar continued working at Triangle Ice and even gained ten, much needed pounds. He also continued to help Dovie around the house and with the bills. Attending church and reading the Bible, however, remained low on his list of priorities. Rebecca enjoyed listening to his childhood stories even though they were few. He encouraged her to be creative with her imagination. Many days Rebecca sat in the swing behind the flower shop imagining herself and her daddy fishing, riding bikes, and throwing a football around.

Rebecca changed in noticeable ways that winter, too. She packed up her baby dolls in a Chiquita banana box her mama brought home from Fletcher's Grocery Store. Her earrings got bigger while her waist got smaller, and what used to be bangs were now breeze backs. She exchanged pink gingham curtains and bedspread for huge hot pink, green, and orange flowers unarranged on a purple comforter. The word LOVE, in white wooden letters, hung above her bed on freshly painted walls of lime green. As far as she was concerned, she was finished with sixth grade and the preteen years, even though, technically, she still had a few weeks to go. Thirteen was coming, and gone were the days of fearing to ask for what she wanted.

"Can I have a boy-girl birthday party this year?" Rebecca asked as she set down the wheelbarrow full of peat moss.

"Rebecca, you need to ask your mama, not me."

"I mean, can I have it here?"

"Why didn't you say so? You know I don't care if you have it here as long as your mama says you can have the party. A boy-girl party is a lot different from the girl parties you usually have."

"I know. Since I *am* going to be a teenager, the girls and I started thinking it's time we included the guys in on the fun. You know they're not nearly as immature as they used to be; they hardly talk about passing gas or anything embarrassing anymore. Mary and David are even going together."

"Going together where?"

"No, they're going together. Period. They're going…Oh, I guess you used to say going steady. Mary and David are going steady."

"Okay. Now are you wanting to have it on Friday or Saturday night?"

"My birthday is on Friday this year, so why don't we have it then? That's two weeks from this Friday by the way."

"Well, your mama has the final say-so. If she says yes, you got some planning to do. Like what are ya'll going do for four or five hours? You can't jump on the trampoline that long."

"I know. We'll eat and talk, play spin the bottle, kiss and tell, dance. Stuff like that."

"Lord have mercy, I got to talk to Marie about this. She'll have to help chaperone. You done gone and mixed the peanut butter with the jelly now." Lottie got up from the patch of ground in front of the daffodils. "No, peanut butter wasn't good enough by itself, now we got to go mixing it," she said as she wiped the dirt off her hands. "I was just getting used to the girl parties. I'm going to call your mama."

Rebecca mixed the peat moss with the dirt in the flower beds. She hummed a tune that had been in her head all day. Yep, she was on top of the world, looking down on creation.

All the invited girls were coming to the party. The boys were still unsure about the whole party thing, so only a few came right out with it and said they were coming. Rebecca made Patricia and Mary promise they would not mention the word "dance" to the guys. She was certain that would scare all of them away. Of course, David would be there because he was going with Mary, but a dozen girls couldn't spin one bottle with one guy. They desperately needed diversity.

The weather cooperated with temperatures in the low seventies and no rain in sight. The menu included hot dogs which would be placed on the grill just before six o'clock, chips, Pepsi, and a double chocolate butter cream birthday cake.

Mary and Patricia, giddy and giggly, arrived just after four to help blow up balloons and hang purple streamers. By now, Lottie was used to the get-togethers and didn't mind the noise or commotion. She sent Marie out to the garden to drape Dovie's Christmas lights on the shrubs and along the fence. This would be a surprise even to Rebecca. Flowers were arranged, as usual, and placed in noticeable locations throughout the house. Lottie was positive not a single stem would be admired but that didn't stop her from displaying them. After all, what was a party without flowers?

Lottie smelled the sweet perfume before her eyes ever saw the girl who wore it; then Rebecca stepped into the living room. She looked good, smelled good, and had spent way too much time on herself. But, it was her birthday and she was thirteen. To Lottie she was the most beautiful young lady in the world.

"Fifteen minutes until arrival time, Miss Lottie," she said, fluffing her recently cut hair. "Where are Mary and Patricia?"

"They're on the back porch setting up the disc jockey area. Between your record player and Mary's eight-track tape player it's gonna be American Bandstand and Soul Train together for the first time."

"Oh, I've got to go see! They were supposed to bring all their disco records!" Rebecca was gone before Lottie had time to ask her about disco. She knew all about Marvin Gaye and just enough about Barry White to blush, but disco? She wasn't sure about all that. Then came a knock at the door.

"Well, come on in, you good-looking fellas. Ya'll at the right house?" Lottie asked.

David said they were; he was the only one who knew for sure. "It's nice to finally get to come to one of your parties, Miss Lottie. Where do you want us to put the gifts?"

"Follow me. We'll put them on the coffee table in here."

Rebecca, Mary, and Patricia walked in from the back porch, giggling at the sight of Tony, Doug, Eddie and Wayne. Before the boys had time to turn completely red, there was another knock at the door.

By six o'clock, all twenty-three young people were standing around talking and enjoying themselves in a self-conscious-sort-of-way. The only ones who laughed out loud were the ones who meant to, and when someone in the group wanted to move to another spot, the group moved together, as a whole, like paperclips pulled by a magnet across paper.

When it was dark enough, Marie plugged in the Christmas lights for a beautiful effect in the garden. Patricia squealed that the back yard now looked like a real disco club, except for the lack of a mirrored ball hanging overhead.

The party appeared to be a success.

By eight o'clock the kids were louder and less self-conscious. The lower lighting helped.

"Why are all the guys on one end of the garden and the girls on the other end?" Lottie asked Marie.

"I don't know. I was wondering the same thing." Marie got up and walked across the yard.

Rebecca stood with her hands on her hips, obviously not happy. "Well, Wayne brought his eight-track tape of C.W. McCall, so all they've been listening to is the "Convoy". They're talking in code: Rubber Duck and Pigpen, negatory and big 10-4. It's so childish."

"Well, maybe you should turn your music up louder. That would be the mature thing to do. They may get the hint and start wandering over this way," Marie suggested.

"That's a good idea, Mama. Thanks."

Marie went back and sat beside Lottie.

"Well, what's going on?" Lottie asked.

"The boys want to listen to trucking tunes and the girls want to dance. Not much changes in life, does it?"

"That must be a white thing, because no black man I ever knew would be listening to trucking tunes, especially if all them fine ladies were that close by wanting to dance."

All of a sudden KC and the Sunshine Band livened up the garden with a little "Shake Your Booty" which Lottie had never heard in her life. "What in the world are they saying?" she yelled. She didn't really need to know what they were saying because she heard the words loud and clear. "I'm going in for a Booty Powder—I mean a Goody Powder. Do you want anything?"

Marie shook her head.

The telephone was ringing when Lottie walked into the kitchen. "It's probably the po-lice talking about disturbing the peace and-all-and-everthang," she mumbled to herself. "Hello," she hollered into the phone.

"Lottie, this is Dovie. I know I done heard the O'Jays on that "Love Train." Now "Shake Your Booty" is making its way over the fence. What's going on?"

"It's the boy-girl party I told you and Edgar about, remember? I got a ton of 13-year-olds, and I got to keep an eye on things. Let me go."

"Hey, I got grans a little older than that. You want me to come over and show them some dance moves?"

"Don't you dare bring yourself over here, Dovie Williams. Dovie? Hello?" Lottie walked to the front door with gritted teeth; her clinched jaw kept the dentures in place. She opened the door and there stood Dovie, looking like Patti La Belle. "Well, thank God you had enough sense to put a robe on," Lottie said. When her eyes finished the tour, she stared at Dovie's feet. "What in the world are you doing with them platforms on? You think we got a real dance floor out back?"

"Well, I can't move and slide in my house shoes, can I? Get out of my way. I'm going to shake my booty a little bit."

"A little bit? Remember what all you carrying back there. They got signs for that at the hardware store. And what about your arthritis, Dovie Williams?"

"What about it?"

Lottie watched Dovie's blue chenille robe bang from side to side. She took a Goody Powder and walked back outside.

"You got "Fire" by the Ohio Players? That's perfect for learning the Bump." Dovie's raised arms swayed from side to side; her fingers snapped to the beat.

"Yes, ma'am, we've got that one," Mary said.

"Good. Now before you play it, let me get a couple of you girls over here beside me. I'm gonna show ya'll how to do the Bump."

Lottie watched from the steps of the back porch, certain the rescue squad would have to be called as soon as Dovie started bumping these seventy-five-pound girls across the yard. "Dovie!" she yelled from the steps. "You remember now, you ain't dancing with Big Daddy John-John from church. These just little tiny things."

"Lottie, I know what I'm doing. I told you I got grans of my own. Me and Edgar practice our disco every Saturday night. Now watch and learn." Dovie smiled as she looked over the group of girls.

"Just think, a ninety-something-year-old woman is teaching us the hottest dance around," Mary said to Patricia.

"You know all black women can dance, don't you?"

"Oh, yeah. They can dance to white music, too. Probably even country."

The W.C. McCall fan club broke up as soon as Dovie started shaking it loose. Even Marie found herself moving her hips from side to side, ever so gently. "Brick House," "Boogie Nights," "Car Wash," "The Hustle," Dovie grooved to them all.

Lottie made her way through the dance maze and yelled into Dovie's ear, "I know you're working up a sweat but if you take that robe off and I'm gonna take pictures. I'll plaster them from Fletcher's all the way to the church bulletin board. You understand me?"

"What's wrong with you? Just because I like to dance don't mean I ain't got no decency. Go on inside and take a spoon of Rock and Rye."

After the third Goody Powder, Lottie knew of only one thing that would help calm her nerves. She sat at the piano and softly played "Nearer My God to Thee."

Since I've been writing, a strange thing has happened. I start talking to Rebecca about something that happened a long time ago and I don't feel my throat close up or my eyes start to water. I can tell a story with a smile. Remember good times like they just happened. I call that amazing! I also call my writing abilities amazing. When I get a pencil in my hand, feels like it moves on its own. Rebecca says it's because I'm a writer. She said, "You must be a writer, Miss Lottie. My pencil don't move nothing like yours."

Chapter Fourteen

Nadine glanced up from her desk and greeted Edgar with a thin-lipped smile. "Aren't you glad it's Friday?"

"Man, yeah." He started toward the warehouse when she spoke again.

"Mr. Dempsey wants to see you in his office, first thing."

"Thanks." He pushed the door open, stepped into the canteen, put his supper in the refrigerator, then walked to Mr. Dempsey's office. *The last review I got was good. They've all been good. Stop getting yourself worked up.* He continued down the hall and past the water fountain. He swallowed, wiped his damp hands on his pants, and tapped on the door.

Mr. Dempsey's voice sounded upbeat and friendly. "Come in, Edgar. You doing okay today?"

"Yes, sir. Doing fine. Nadine said you wanted to see me." He sat down in the chair Mr. Dempsey pulled out and looked at his watch.

"I'll make it quick. There are a couple of things we need to discuss. The first one is, and I'm sure it's no surprise to you, we are finally at a point in production where we have the need to open some permanent positions." He leaned back in his chair as he held Edgar's file in his hand. "Let's see. You started with us in the spring of '72, right?"

"Yes, sir."

"So, you've been on temporary status for a few years. Not many people would have stuck with us that long. I appreciate your patience and steady job performance."

"Thank you. Well, I don't have a wife and kids like most of the guys here, so not having insurance never bothered me." He smiled and shrugged his shoulders. "I'm never sick."

"I'm just glad you stayed with us. Now, this is where I offer you a permanent, forty-hour-a-week position. You'll still have to be on second shift, though. Does that work for you?"

"Yes, sir."

"Good. Another plus besides immediate insurance benefits is you'll get a raise. You'll be making $4.05 an hour instead of $3.80. Your increase will be in your check two weeks from now."

Edgar smiled and nodded. "That's great."

Mr. Dempsey stepped to the front of his desk and halfway sat on the corner of it with one foot on the floor and the other swinging in Edgar's direction. "Would you like something to drink? A Pepsi?"

"No, I'm fine."

His boss rubbed his hands together, clapped once, then rested them, folded, in his lap. "The second item I wanted to discuss with you is a little more personal."

Edgar's heart pounded an extra beat inside his chest. *Only a few people know I'm a recovering alcoholic.* His mind raced with questions while he watched Mr. Dempsey's mouth form the next sentence in slow motion.

"We had a city council meeting last week, and someone there told me about the little mishap you had over at the cemetery." He cleared his throat. "Now, you are going to AA meetings now, right?"

"Yes." Edgar wondered where the conversation was going.

"Good for you. And I also learned that Lottie Johnson is your cousin. Isn't that odd how lives and situations are intermingled? I mean, the council meeting was about the town wanting to purchase a certain someone's property and that certain someone just happens to be your cousin. And you just happen to work for me and you're offered a permanent position at Triangle Ice and also a substantial raise." Mr. Dempsey hopped off the desk and walked slowly to the sunlit window, his back to Edgar. "But the incident at the cemetery and AA meetings, well, that does send up some red flags." He turned around, then quickly appeared in front of Edgar. He rested his hands on the arms of Edgar's chair. "However, if you thought there was a chance you could persuade a certain someone to sell her property, I feel quite sure those red flags could be lowered. You see, Edgar, there is a real need for that property. Who knows? I may even purchase it if it goes on the market. The bottom line here is you need this job and Mt. Brayden needs that property."

Edgar scrambled for something to say.

"Do you want to think about it over the weekend?"

He wanted to tell Mr. Dempsey what he could do with his job but decided against it. The truth was he needed this job. What would Lottie and Dovie think? If Lottie agreed to sell, she would be financially secure and live in a newer home without repair needs. How could that be wrong? No, he couldn't tell Mr. Dempsey to shove it. He needed to think this thing through. "I'll give you an answer Monday afternoon."

"Great." Mr. Dempsey held out his hand to Edgar.

Dazed, Edgar walked out of the office and past his work station. He needed to wash his hands.

"Hey. What are you up to this morning?"

"Cleaning out the refrigerator. What about you?" Lottie asked.

"I'm supposed to climb under the house and check the duct work for Dovie. It won't be long until the cold weather sets in."

"How about coming over and checking mine, too. If you got time."

"Okay. I needed to stop by anyway. I wanted to run something past you."

Ten minutes later Edgar sat across from Lottie in her living room. Lottie thought his speech, which he obviously memorized and rehearsed aloud in front of a mirror, was convincing and well thought out. She was also certain Edgar removed all feelings of shame, guilt, and wrongdoing by adding, "I'm doing what's best for both of us."

She listened as he told her that she was at an age where a low-maintenance home would be best. After all, he couldn't be expected to take care of her house and Dovie's. He had a job which required a lot of hours; maybe one day he'd remarry; what if his job ended and he needed to move again? Next, he reminded her how dangerous old wiring could be to a home as old as hers. This place would go up in flames in minutes, he said. Then, Edgar covered the obvious reasons why she should consider selling her home: money, money and more money.

Lottie rubbed the back of her neck. "You know money has never meant that much to me no way Edgar. Plus, I've saved my whole life."

"But have you ever stopped to think about how fast your money would go if you were placed in retirement home? Not far enough, I'm sure. If you sold this place and bought something else—new or newer, maintenance-free, beautiful, and comfortable—your investment would only increase in value. Don't you see the advantages, Lottie? And just think, you'd never have to feel like a second-class citizen again. You could finally snub your nose at the people of Mt. Brayden."

Lottie listened to him without interrupting or rolling her eyes or huffing. She saw relief on Edgar's face when he finished. She thought for a few minutes longer. Horizontal and vertical lines were left on the arm of the velour recliner where she rubbed, absentmindedly, with her fingernail.

"First, let me tell you how much it means to me to know that you care about my safety and well-being. I've never thought about my home being a fire hazard. And I've never considered how much it would cost to stay in a nursing home for a long period of time. As far as the money goes, you're right there, too. I would have a new home paid for, plus money in the bank making more money."

She rested her head on the back of the recliner. "You know, it would be nice to live in a new place and have air conditioning and soft, thick carpet, maybe even one of them fancy doorbells that plays sophisticated music when you push the button." She smiled. "But what you haven't considered, Edgar, is my garden. It's like my family; it's grown and changed. Every morning, season after season, it's been there for me. And because of my garden, I just can't picture an ugly brick building with lights and asphalt and noise scattered all around it."

She pushed herself from the recliner and walked around to the window behind her. Hazy pinks, yellows, reds, and blues teased her through white sheers—calling her name like children eager to play. She pulled the curtains back and revealed their rich, vivid color. Her body soaked up the tones like artist's paper, while their fragrance traveled through the window screen. She imagined their taste on her tongue: blueberry, lemon, cherry, and cotton candy; the feel of their velvet petals between her fingers. Then the grip of her hand loosened and the curtains fell.

She told Edgar about the flower pressing and memory cards. "As far as me snubbing the people in town, I've worked through all that with the cards. I know it sounds odd, but God gave me the idea. It began as a way to preserve flowers from my garden, but then it became a way—a real, practical way I could move past bad feelings, anger, and rejection and reach out with love to the people of this town. I've learned that they're human just like me. They have disappointments, and sorrows, and joys. And they can hurt others, just like I can. But the day I began to put myself into their lives and into their day-to-day happenings, I began to care about them."

Edgar lowered his head and sighed. His elbows rested on his knees and his head hung heavy between his shoulders. "You know it's unlikely that your house will catch on fire because of faulty wiring. I mean, the wiring may be fine. I don't know. And as far as the nursing home goes, you'll be plugging away in that garden into the next century. You'd only be about ninety years old. Just forget all that stuff I said."

"I will not. All the stuff you brought up is just what I need to be thinking about. It shows that you care, Edgar."

"Not really."

"What do you mean, not really?" Lottie watched Edgar's hands wipe the sweat from his forehead. She remembered thinking his eyes looked weak and strained when he walked in. "Is something wrong?"

He lifted his head and looked up at her. "Actually, I'm glad to say that nothing is wrong, now. Lottie, I came in here this morning to try and convince you to sell your property so I wouldn't lose my job at Triangle."

"What?"

"Mr. Dempsey offered me a permanent position and a good raise if I could persuade you to sell. If I refuse his offer, I may lose my job. I know all the reasons I gave you for selling were good ones, but my motive was rotten. I'm ashamed of myself. I'm sorry, Lottie."

Her hands smoothed the fabric of her dress over her knees. She watched Edgar stand and walk across the room for a tissue. Surprisingly, her heart was at peace.

"Edgar, what we have both witnessed here this morning is God doing what only God can do, and that is change hearts. You came in here to do one thing but you ended up doing something else. A few minutes ago I wanted to tear your backside up but I decided, like you, to follow my heart. Now I know that if I do decide to sell, my life will still be full and blessed—maybe even more than it is now. And don't worry about your job. God's on the throne, not Mr. Dempsey."

Lottie put on her garden gloves and grabbed the pruning shears from the table on the back porch.

She fed the hydrangeas and thought of Rebecca. *This is her favorite flower. She was only seven when we planted it.* She stopped pouring the liquid. *Seven years ago? Where did that sweet, clingy little girl go? She was just here helping me, getting in my way.*

It was Monday afternoon and Rebecca's arrival from school brought Lottie back to the present. "I'm so glad you decided to come over today," Lottie said to her. "I wanted to tell you about the nice lady I met yesterday after church. I see her every time I go into the library but I never talked to her until yesterday. Her name is Ann. She's the librarian."

Rebecca twisted the stem off an apple. She took a big bite and sat down on the ground.

"We talked and talked, like we'd known each other all our lives. And she has the best sense of humor. She had me laughing so hard I was afraid my dentures might slip. She told me she had noticed all the flower and gardening books I checked out. Then she asked me about myself and before I knew it, I was telling her about you and Marie, the flower pressing, the memory cards, and your mama's shop."

"You told her about all of that? I can't believe it."

"I know. I surprised myself. And what really surprised me is when I told her about the flower pressing and the memory cards, she told me that would make a good book!"

"A book!" Rebecca smiled. "Sounds like you have a new friend."

"Maybe. How about something to drink?"

Together they walked to the house and into the kitchen. Rebecca pull the chair closer to the table and rest her chin in her hand. After Lottie filled the glasses with lemonade she continued. "I think Ann could be a real friend. But you know, won't nobody ever take your place or your mama's. Some things you can discuss with friends, but some things…well, you can't talk to anyone about except your family.

"I'm in a strange place, Rebecca; I'm restless. I go from the bedroom to the living room, sort of like I'm dragging myself around. I've never been this way before. Do you understand what I'm saying?"

She thought for a minute. "I think so. Remember when I changed my room around and painted the walls, and I decided to pack my dolls up and put them in the attic? I felt strange. I wanted to make the change, but in some ways I didn't."

Lottie nodded. "All of my life I've been comfortable here. I used to think I could stay in this house and piddle in the garden forever; didn't matter if I ever got out or saw another soul. But now it seems like I'm ready to go somewhere all the time. I'm talking to people at Fletcher's and over at the post office. I've even been over to see Dovie again this week. I don't know what's wrong with me. I feel like I'm turning into one of those people I never liked. The ones who talk too much."

"Hey, Miss Lottie. I think I just figured us both out. I think we've outgrown ourselves." Lottie felt a tingle work its way up her spine.

Ann helped me find a great book on transplanting flowers and shrubs. I just decided to do a little research. I guess in this journal it's okay to make confessions. Here's one: used to I wouldn't have wanted to make friends with someone like Ann—a white woman who's a librarian. I doubt if I would have even thought to smile at her if I passed her in Fletcher's. I hate to admit it, but I think I was a snob. I thought they were the snobs, looking down on me. But I guess it was me looking down on myself and thinking they were looking down on me, too. It's amazing how different people are when you see them through new eyes.

I've seen Edgar through new eyes, too. He has a conscience and he has a good heart. When he used to drink, I considered all of his moral character to be lost. I was wrong. I'm glad God doesn't think like I do.

Chapter Fifteen

After the supper dishes were washed and dried, she asked Marie to follow her to the bedroom. They sat down on the edge of the bed and faced each other. "Let me turn the lamp on so I can see your face," Lottie said. "Now, that's better."

"This must be something important. I've never known you to ask Rebecca to let us talk in private."

"I hope I can tell you all of it. I'll try my best...well, my dreams are usually in color, but last night the dream was different. It started out in color: blues, greens, and reds, and sunlight filtering in like stage lighting on a movie set. I just stood there, looking around. I couldn't move. I was outside in the garden, but the flowers and colors were so bright, they didn't look real. I took a deep breath and then I touched some pink peonies and yellow roses. They felt like satin between my fingers. Their scent was strong and sweet.

"I remember I floated to the corner of the garden where the Don Juan rose bush was. It looked like it was on fire, and the ruby red roses were the tips of the flames. I reached out to pick one, but before I could, a flower was placed between my fingers. Inside myself I knew who put it there." She reached over and pulled a tissue from the box on the night stand. "Jerome stood in front of me. He was dressed in a glowing white shirt and creased black pants. His shirt was tucked in and his black belt ended with a shiny gold buckle. Seeing him took my breath away.

"Then Jerome reached out to take my other hand. That's when I looked down. I realized that my hands were not in color like Jerome's or like the rest of the dream. The rose was blood red, but my arms, and my dress, my legs, and my shoes, all were gray.

"I wanted Jerome to explain it to me and then his smile faded. He said, 'Lottie, my love, no more grave clothes.'"

Lottie felt Marie's arms wrapped tight around her. She tried to talk but couldn't. Marie went into the bathroom for a wet washcloth.

Lottie let the cool cloth rest on her eyelids before she continued.

"Jerome's words melted me like hot wax; they will stay with me forever. He freed me with those four simple words."

She lifted her head and took a deep breath. "Every year, layer after layer, those grave clothes were my protection, thick and hard as metal. Marie, I've learned to live with sadness and I admit I hid in its protection. Now I'm expected to strip? Bare? Naked? But I keep telling myself that Jerome was right. Grief has robbed me of life too long. I thought I was free before because of being able to read so well and through all of the learning over the years with Rebecca." She took Marie's hands in hers. "The Lord never lets his children stop learning or growing or changing."

I might not be able to write down what I remember. My heart is beating so fast. No, I can't write about it now. Maybe I'll be able to after Rebecca comes over. She's my medicine.

Rebecca did help me today. She told me about how upset she was that she and Mary argued again at school. I told her I understood, but still she wanted to explain it to me. That poor child had the weight of the world on her when she started talking to me. Then when she unloaded all that heartache, she was light as a biscuit. I knew then that I had to write down what happened to my precious Jerome and our little baby girl.

It happened on a Saturday about four o'clock. I know because me and Mama had just finished cleaning Mrs. Radcliff's house. As we came up the hill and crossed over onto Kelly Street, I saw Daddy standing on the porch waving his arms. I told Mama that Daddy was waving to us. She said oh, he's just carrying on some nonsense. But I told her, no Mama, it looks like something's wrong. I ran to the porch and saw that Daddy was crying. His eyes were so red they looked like they had blood in them. When he reached out and grabbed hold of me, I knew something terrible had happened to my baby. He was crying so hard he couldn't talk to me. I pushed away and said Daddy, tell me what happened to my baby. But he just shook his head and kept on crying. Mama was on the porch now and she got hold of Daddy and she shook him hard. He had one arm around me and one around Mama like he was holding us up, but we were the ones holding him up. I remember Mama saying, you got to tell us what happened.

Jerome and Wyonnia had been to see uncle HK, Daddy's brother. They were going to get some iris bulbs for me because uncle HK had thinned out his beds. Jerome knew how much I wanted those irises so he promised me he would go Saturday and get them. Little Wy wanted to go with her daddy. She was only three; her daddy was her sunshine. The old man who hit them must have lost control of his car. He died later that day. Jerome and Wy died right there on Salter's Creek Road. My world was gone.

❖

Chapter Sixteen

Rebecca threw the outdated dress on the bed. No one understood. This was her first high school dance and she couldn't go in just any old thing. Mary and Patricia had driven all the way across the state line to shop in Asheville. They would be the best-dressed girls there. This didn't make Rebecca feel any better. Ever since Mary and David broke up, Mary and Patricia snubbed her. *Is it my fault we're a couple now?* She walked over to the wicker chair by the window and plopped down. *Well, they'll just have to get over it. David and I have known each other since first grade. Just because he doesn't love Mary anymore doesn't mean he can't love me.*

She looked out the window at the dogwood tree below. Pink and white blossoms created a thick, quilted covering. *If Mama can drive me to Greenville this Saturday, I can buy a new dress. Something different. And I won't have to worry about seeing the same thing on five other girls. I'll walk to the shop and ask her.*

All Rebecca heard at school, at home, and around town was talk of the recession, gas prices up to eighty-two cents per gallon, and conserve energy, conserve energy, conserve energy. She rolled her eyes. *Right now all I care about is getting a new dress and some Candies so I can dance, dance, dance better on the dance floor.*

She swung the heavy door open so hard that the brass bells hitting the glass were louder than the bells ringing. She saw her mama whirl around from behind the counter to see what the commotion was.

"Don't let the door slam, Rebecca," she said sharply.

"I'm sorry, Mama. I wasn't thinking. Could we go to Greenville this Saturday so I can get a new dress and shoes for the school dance?"

"Honey, I can't go anywhere Saturday because of the Biggers' wedding."

"That's great! Now I'll never be able to get a new dress. I've saved up my money and everything."

"What about Lottie? She could ride with you."

"I don't think Miss Lottie will want to ride with me all the way to Greenville. She's made it clear that she doesn't trust any driver under the age of forty-five. I'm not even sure I'd know how to get there."

"Well, you should ask her anyway. Tell her you'll drive slow, which is the truth."

"Yes, ma'am. I'll walk over there and ask her."

Lottie was walking through the living room with her hands full of memory cards when Rebecca knocked on the screen door.

"Come on in, gal."

"Miss Lottie, please say yes."

"Girl, I never agree to anything without knowing the details. Now start all over." She put the cards on the coffee table and sat down on the couch.

"The school dance is next week and I need to go shopping; you know there's nothing but Kmart around here. Plus, I don't want to wear the same style dress that someone else is wearing. Anyway, I need an adult to ride with me to Greenville Saturday. Mama can't go because of the Biggers' wedding."

"Oh, Lord. I have dreaded this day."

"Miss Lottie, I've been driving for almost six months. I haven't had a wreck yet and I don't drive over the speed limit. What's there to be scared of?"

"Screeching tires and my head flying through the windshield!"

Rebecca couldn't help but laugh. "Please, ride with me. I have to get a dress without the Kmart label and a pair of shoes with the Candies stamp. This is my first high school dance!"

Lottie let out a long sigh. "I'll ride with you if we can leave early before the traffic gets heavy, if you promise to drive slow, and if you're the only teenager in the car."

Rebecca wrapped both arms tight around Lottie's neck and squeezed. "I promise! Thank you, Miss Lottie. I'll be here to pick you up at nine o'clock Saturday morning."

Lottie showered and dressed quickly so she could read her Bible and spend some time praying—loud and on her knees. Riding in the car with a child driving was a serious matter.

After spending time with the Lord, Lottie felt at peace about the drive. She even thought about buying herself something new while she was out. *Maybe some gardening gloves or a new broom.* She heard a car horn. "What in the world is that child doing blowing the horn for me? Don't she know you don't do things like that?" She shook her head and gathered up her pocketbook and straw hat. She walked to the car, then pulled the door open. Her tall frame folded neatly like an accordion as she lowered herself into the front seat.

"I hope I'm not too early, Miss Lottie. I wanted to beat the rush."

She looked at Rebecca. "That's okay. Just remember you don't need to speed." Lottie lowered her head and raised her eyebrows. "How fast you planning on going?"

"Well, that all depends on the speed limit."

"No it don't. Just because the sign says sixty-five don't mean you got to go sixty-five. Forty-five is a safe speed on any highway."

The warm air billowed through the open car windows. Lottie decided to wear her straw hat in the car so her hair wouldn't get messed up. Rebecca turned on the radio. A loud thumping song roared through the speakers. Rebecca took one hand off the steering wheel to snap her fingers with the beat.

"You know what this song is? 'That's the Way I Like it' by KC and the Sunshine Band." She kept snapping her fingers and then she started moving her shoulders from side to side.

Lottie looked at Rebecca in total disbelief. She gripped the door handle and closed her eyes just long enough to take a deep breath. "Well, that's not the way I like it, now turn that junk off and concentrate on the road! My life is hanging by dental floss, and you're wanting to dance and drive at the same time. No, ma'am. Turn it off."

"Well, what if we roll up the windows, then I can turn down the radio."

"I thought you wanted to save on gas and not run the air conditioner."

"I'd rather listen to the radio and lose out on the gas. You know it's thirty miles to Greenville."

"Yeah, believe me, I know; thirty long miles." Lottie rolled up her window. "Can you at least find a station that plays Aretha Franklin or Smokey Robinson?"

"Who? Miss Lottie, you can turn the station where you want it. I've never heard of those people before."

Aretha Franklin? "R-E-S-P-E-C-T"? "No, you go ahead and keep it here. I'll try to close my eyes and relax." *Forgive me Lord. I have failed as a black woman. This child has spent*

years with me and I never exposed her to any kind of soulful
heritage. I'm so ashamed. Not a word about Dinah Washington
or Mahalia Jackson. Oh, well. It's too late now. Earth Wind
and Fire, Parliament; what kind of names are those anyway?
What's the world coming to?

Rebecca was careful to keep her speed down to fifty miles
an hour. With the slower speed, the windows rolled up, and
the music turned down, Lottie was able to relax and ungrip
the door handle. Before she knew it, the trail of tears was over
and she was sitting, sound and in one piece, in front of Belk
department store.

Since Lottie only wore shifts and dresses, and their only
difference being the color of the cotton, she was unprepared
for the adventure that lay ahead. The first mission for Rebecca
was to find *the* dress. And in order to find *the* dress, you had
to wade through every other *ordinary* dress. That took time.

Lottie soon realized it made no difference if she thought
the dress was beautiful and perfect on Rebecca or not. It made
no difference whatsoever. None. She understood that Rebecca
only asked what she thought about a dress simply to hear
voices; someone speaking English.

She even tested her theory: when Rebecca asked what she
thought of the red and white fluffy dress, Lottie told her she
looked like a piece of peppermint candy at Christmas time.

Rebecca said, "Yeah," and kept looking at herself in the
mirror. "So, you really like this one, Miss Lottie?"

"I love that one. I think you need to buy it; it's perfect."

"Well, I don't know. Maybe it's too flashy. You know, red
and white."

And so the search continued. Lottie was beginning to enjoy
the hunt though. It was like she was invisible. She'd make
crazy comments to Rebecca without ever being heard: no, I

hate that one; you look like a pear; that one makes you look like a clown.

Finally, Rebecca tried on a white eyelet ruffled skirt with a matching peasant top. It really did look great on Rebecca but Lottie knew better than to say so.

"Well, it looks okay. If you want to look like a snowman," Lottie said under her breath.

"A snowman? That's not a very nice thing to say. What's the matter with you?"

She laughed. "I'm just playing with you. I think that outfit looks beautiful. Is that the one?"

"Yes! I love it!"

"Thank God."

"Now all we have to do is find some shoes. I want a pair of Candies; everybody's wearing them plus the name is stamped on the side."

"Hold up. Let me get this straight: you don't want a dress with the K-mart label that nobody can see but you do want a pair of shoes with the Candies stamp that everybody *can* see?"

"Yes ma'am. Candies are...well, I don't know but K-mart is...well, just never mind. I'm fifteen, I know what I'm talking about."

"Okay. I just wanted to clear that up. I forgot you're fifteen." Lottie smiled.

Around one o'clock they finished eating at Burger King and agreed it was time to head back to Mt. Brayden. Rebecca was especially excited about her new outfit and talked nonstop most of the way home. She thanked Lottie repeatedly for going with her. Lottie felt she should be the one thanking Rebecca and was glad she came along for the ride.

Lottie gathered up her notebook, adjusted her straw hat, and headed out the front door. Her steps were light and bouncy. She looked down at the gleaming white tennis shoes Rebecca convinced her to buy on their trip to Greenville. Lottie was so used to the brown leather brogans it took a lot of persuasion from Rebecca, but decidedly, Lottie agreed. Now she was glad she had bought them; her legs were lighter and her feet felt like they were walking on cushions.

"Hey, Miss Lottie!" David yelled as he waved in the passing car.

Lottie smiled and waved back. Leander pressed clothes at Swift's Dry Cleaners so Lottie stopped by and caught up on the recent prayer requests. Leander had a son in prison, a great-nephew in the Black Panthers, and the rest of the family in the Methodist church. Leander was Holiness. That was plenty to pray for.

After she left Swift's, Lottie walked toward Main, then stopped in front of Biggers' dress shop. She had some extra time so she went in. She had met Lucille Biggers when she dropped off Patricia for one of the sleep-overs. Even though Lottie knew Fontaine Biggers' daughter-in-law was not the same kind of woman she was, her heart still beat quick when she reached for the handle of the door and pushed it open.

"Well, hello, Lottie. I haven't seen you in a while. Have you been doing all right?" Mrs. Biggers asked.

"I sure have and you?"

"Oh, we're doing fine. Can I help you with anything in particular today?"

"No, I was just on my way to meet Marie and I thought I'd see what pretty things you have. Rebecca is at the age where she's choosey about her clothes. We drove all the way

188 Sandi Morgan Denkers

to Greenville weekend before last to get her an outfit for the dance."

"I know what you mean. Patricia is the same way. I don't have much for the teenagers to choose from, but I hope to change all that soon. I've decided to carry some dresses and pant suits for young ladies. Even though I've always carried prom dresses, sometimes they just need a special outfit, like for the dance."

"Well, I'll be sure to tell Rebecca to stop by soon and have a look around. I may be sorry I did though."

"Thank you. And thank you too for all the special parties you've given Rebecca over the years. That's all Patricia and Mary remember as fun from junior high. And your neighbor, Mrs. Williams, it's because of her the girls started to dance in the first place; Patricia would have been too shy to try it any other way."

Lottie felt her face warm up. "Yes, Dovie still talks about that, too." *I'm still trying to forget.*

"If you need any help with anything, just let me know. Nice seeing you again, Lottie," Mrs. Biggers said.

Lottie browsed through the sale racks and then looked at the hats and scarves. Suddenly, she remembered her meeting with Marie. She surprised herself at how quickly her apprehension disappeared. For the first time in her life, Lottie had lost track of time. She hurried out the door and down the street. Odelia stepped out of the post office and wanted to talk. "Not now, Odelia. Save it for later."

Marie opened the door before Lottie finished knocking. "I hurried home as soon as I closed up. I thought I might have missed you."

"I stopped by Biggers' for a minute and we got to talking," Lottie said, coolly.

Marie's eyebrows lifted. "Have you started shopping in there?"

Lottie crossed her arms across her chest. "No, but I plan to one day. Especially with Rebecca's taste in clothes. Lucille Biggers is a nice lady, nothing like Fontaine."

"Yea, Lucille is nice. Well, tell me what's so important to bring you down here on a Saturday afternoon," Marie said as she sat down on the couch.

Lottie clutched her notebook, took a deep breath, then sat down beside her. "I have decided to sell my house and land."

"What?" she said. "Well, tell me about it."

"Marie, for over a year now, I've felt strange inside. I don't even know how to explain it, except that I've felt restless. The house started to feel like a place I was visiting, instead of my home. Over and over again I'd hear Mr. Radcliff's words about selling and the more I thought about it and weighed the options, the more I could see that God had opened a wonderful door of opportunity for me. I've listed the advantages of selling, and as you can see here, it would only be to my benefit to sell." Lottie handed the opened notebook to Marie.

Marie read the list to herself, nodding her head in approval. "You would definitely get a large selling price which would allow you to buy a great new or newer home. At your age, the least amount of maintenance you have to worry about, the better. You most certainly do deserve to live in a beautiful neighborhood. And one of the most important points here, I think, is the fact that you can have your garden transplanted to your new home site. This all sounds wonderful, Lottie. I'm so excited."

"I knew you would be, Marie. I've hardly slept a wink in the past two weeks. I never realized, until the dream, just how vacant my life has been. I'm ready to move on. Just the thought of a new house and new garden to work in…well, it's too much for words. And it's like Jerome told me, it's okay to go."

"How many times have I said you deserve more? This is amazing! Now, what can I do to help?"

"You know I don't know anything about buying or selling a house. Mr. Radcliff told me if I ever decided to sell that he would help me. It's not that I don't trust him, it's just that I'd like to have you by my side through this whole process. If I make an appointment to see Mr. Radcliff on Monday, could you come over to the bank?"

"Of course I can. Just let me know. This is so exciting! Wait until Rebecca hears about it. She's over at the Parris' house babysitting the twins right now. Why don't you call over there and tell her?"

"I think I will. I almost told her when we went to Greenville, but I made myself wait. I wanted to talk to you first."

Marie dialed the number and handed the phone to Lottie. Rebecca's shrills of excitement forced Lottie to hold the phone away from her ear.

I had a strange day today. I was going through my closet trying to get together some things for Marie's yard sale. Back in the back I found the box. I haven't opened it in such a long time, probably fifteen years or more. Some people might wonder how I could keep these clothes, but to me they're priceless. These were the last clothes they wore. August the 14th was the day Wy and Jerome died. It was so hot the air was hard to breathe in; it was thick and muggy. Wy had on a little pink-checked jumper.

She didn't have on any shoes because Jerome always carried her on his shoulders when they had to walk a far piece. I feel bad that I haven't washed and pressed the dress for so many years now. Looks like a baby doll dress, but it's my own baby girl's.

Jerome's overalls and light blue work shirt were on the bottom. Laying there like they were resting through the winter like Rebecca said bears do. The clothes—his clothes—it was like they reached out and grabbed me by the throat. I heard my own breath as it rushed into my chest. Why did the sight of his clothes do that to me? Seeing little Wy's dress brought a smile to my face and I smelled it and kissed it. But Jerome's clothes seemed to have life in them. I smelled Jerome; the sweet cologne he used to wear. I saw his dark brown eyes with long eyelashes coming out from around them like flower petals around the center of a black-eyed Susan. I saw his wide grin; his lips shiny from the brushing of his tongue. My mouth watered. It was like he was here with me. Even more real than all the dreams I've had of him. I stepped over from my life here, in this house, to some other place. I didn't do anything else but sit in the floor. That's all I could do. It was like I had company and I never wanted them to leave.

After Jerome and Wyonnia died, Mama and Daddy took care of me the best they could. Most of those days and months are like a blur. I don't know how I lived except Mama would lay her hands on me and pray. I never told Mama this, but I guess she knew all along, I didn't want to live at all. But I did; time passed. God helped me through the flowers. The garden was my reason to get out of bed every morning. Mama always told me how special a garden was. How Jesus chose the garden when he needed to be alone and pray. God knows I do my share of praying on my knees out there. Sometimes my tears water the ground. Sometimes no tears come at all.

Nobody but the Lord knows the sharp turn my heart made after the accident. Before that I used to go through my days knowing the Lord was on my side. I had the faith of Abraham. Then it seemed like I was flung out into a world so far away from God that he couldn't hear me or see me. I thought he left.

Poor uncle HK didn't make it through those days. His death helped me understand a little more about the ways of God. I couldn't believe it when I got the news of him dying. All Daddy could say was Oh God, HK done gone and killed himself. There's extra suffering when someone you love dies by their own hand. The ones left breathing got to find their own way to survive and make it through living still. Uncle HK blamed himself for what happened. Said if it wasn't for him, they never would have been on the road that day. I guess it played over and over in his mind and he couldn't take it no more. The death of a loved one can do that to you. Death is awful fierce. After it cuts those still living into little pieces, grief comes along to watch them bleed.

But I blamed God for them dying, not uncle HK. That's when I realized that God let HK do what he did. Maybe God tried to speak to him and let him know that it wasn't his fault, but the main thing is, he didn't step down from heaven and take that gun out of uncle HK's hand. He didn't stop that gun from shooting. And in the same way, he didn't stop that car from running into my precious Wy and Jerome. So for years I wouldn't ask God for nothing.

Not his safety, or his blessing, or his help. I figured he's God and he's going to do what he wants to do. Mama always said our God is a good God. But I didn't see it that way. Not then. So the years went by.

After about three years, the thick fog that wrapped itself so tight around me started to lift. I was desperate to hear from God again. I didn't have any more answers for what happened than I did to start with, but I didn't care. My heart was barely able to ask with any kind of faith, but there was still a tiny speck of it somewhere deep inside me. I was sitting outside on the front porch. Wasn't doing nothing but rocking. I thought, I can't go on without God being my friend. I had learned to get along without Jerome and Wy and uncle HK. But I was lost without Jesus in my life. I was on a dead-end road in the middle of the night with no strength to walk the other way. I remember saying out loud—and I surprised myself when I heard my voice—I said, show me God, that you haven't left me. As soon as I said it there was something rose up in me and I got excited. I mean I hadn't been excited about anything for three years. I felt a smile come up on my face, just like it walked up the porch steps and invited itself there. The muscles in my face had been frozen in one place for so long that when the smile did come, the muscles were slow to move, like they didn't remember how. All this and nothing had even happened yet. Nothing I could see with my eyes, because they were still shut tight. I remember the sunshine coming in when I slowly opened my eyes. It was so bright, I felt like I'd been closed up in a cave.

Then I saw it. On my dress, just above my knee, was a single drop of blood. It was just as red as a tomato. I touched it; it was wet. I lifted my dress to see where it came from. There was no cut or scratch or anything on my leg. I looked at my hands and arms. I felt my face and my forehead. It came from nowhere. One drop of blood. From that day I never stopped singing "Oh, the Blood of Jesus." In the morning, at noon time, at bedtime, that song was on my lips.

One drop of blood became a bucket full, pouring over me. Just as soon as the weight of one tide left, there was another one. That blood soothed every wound; washed every black stain; filled every crack and crevice that was open and empty. One drop of blood. That's what Jesus gave to me that day so long ago, just sitting on my front porch rocking.

Chapter Seventeen

It was hot and steamy when Lottie arrived at the bank. She looked at her watch then saw Marie's green Monte Carlo pull quickly into the parking lot.

"I could have picked you up on the way," Marie said as she climbed out of the car.

"That's all right. I couldn't sit still no way."

"Well, that's understandable. Listen, I thought of some things last night while I was trying to go to sleep. Let me do most of the talking. If being in business for myself has taught me anything, it's how to bargain and make the most of a good situation. And this is definitely a good situation because you have something someone else wants. You have the upper hand."

"Whatever you say, Marie."

They only had to wait a few minutes before Mr. Radcliff greeted them in the lobby. "Good morning, ladies. Come on in. Can I get you some coffee?"

Neither one wanted coffee so they were quickly ushered into his office and seated in front of his stately mahogany desk. Mr. Radcliff appeared relaxed as he took off his jacket and draped it over the burgundy damask chair. His eyes were a pleasant shade of blue and his smile was soft and genuine.

"I have to tell you, Mrs. Johnson, I was surprised to hear from you this morning." He folded his hands together and rested them on top of the desk. "What can I help you with?"

"I'm just going to come right out with it, Mr. Radcliff. I've decided I do want to sell my house and land. That is if the price is right."

"And if we can agree on some important stipulations," Marie said.

"I can assure you both that every request will be handled with great care and importance. I'm shocked, Mrs. Johnson. It's been so long, and now, well, I just don't know what to say. But, of course, I'll present your requests to the board and we'll do whatever we can to make the deal go through, If you'll excuse me a minute, I'll get my secretary." He leaned over and spoke into the small black box on his desk. "Martha Kate, will you come take notes for us, please?"

Marie waited to begin until the secretary was seated and ready with her notepad. "We've been told the land will appraise for around one hundred fifty thousand dollars. Mrs. Johnson feels this will be a fair price and is willing to sell for at least that amount." She glanced at her notes. "Also, Mrs. Johnson had aluminum siding and replacement windows installed just over four years ago. We would like Habitat for Humanity to be allowed access to any salvageable portions of her home before it's demolished. Lastly, Mrs. Johnson insists on having her entire garden transplanted by a professional landscaper and replanted at her new residence. She requests the city pay for this expense."

Lottie wanted to reach over and hug Marie for coming up with such great ideas but she remained collected. She cleared her throat. "I've got an appointment Thursday to look at a house in the Windsor neighborhood. It has a vacant lot beside it that's also for sale. It would be perfect for my garden."

Marie continued. "So you see, Mr. Radcliff, it's imperative that Mrs. Johnson get top dollar for her land. And she has to be able to take her garden with her."

"I understand," he said. "For as long as the city has wanted to buy this property, I can't see any objections to your requests. And, from what I've been told, you'll probably get more than a hundred and fifty thousand. Is there anything else you want to add, Mrs. Johnson?"

"No, I think we've covered it."

Lottie and Marie thanked Mr. Radcliff for his help. He suggested they get a lawyer to draw up their requests and stipulations. In the meantime, he would present their offer to sell and their requests to the board.

Moments later, Lottie and Marie enjoyed a late breakfast at the Blue Bird Café.

Lottie drifted off to sleep at three in the morning. When her feet hit the floor at seven she felt like she could run a marathon. She was thankful for the stack of memory cards that needed to be finished; working on them would carry her through until lunch, then the pruning and clipping would finish up the remainder of her time. After a cool shower, she would have just enough time to rest in front of the fan with her feet propped up. She could count on Marie to be there at three-twenty-five sharp, leaving them five minutes to drive to 1335 Sherrill Street.

She changed into her blue shift, then cooked grits and eggs for breakfast. *Yes, those memory cards are a lifesaver. I'll be so busy, time will fly by*

Hours later Marie pulled her car over by the curb. Rebecca scooted to the middle and Lottie climbed in beside her. "We knew you couldn't wait for us at the house. I bet Mama a dollar you'd started walking already."

"I've already seen the smirks and I don't want to hear no cracks. Let's go. We got two minutes."

Marie made a U-turn and hurried in the opposite direction. After a short distance and two quick turns, they were there. Mrs. Ivey, the realtor, pulled up behind them.

The moment Lottie walked up the sidewalk, she loved the place. Monkey grass, thick and graceful, seemed to bow as she walked by. The steps and front porch were made of red brick. White columns supported high-pitched gables while moss-green shingle siding wrapped itself around the exterior. The extra wide front door opened to an airy foyer. Straight ahead, the staircase led up to three large bedrooms and two full baths, each freshly painted and wallpapered. To the left of the foyer was the dining room. Lottie saw where the piano would go. She also realized she would have to have new furniture in order to fill up the place. To the right of the foyer was the living room, complete with a fireplace and beautiful walnut-stained mantle. After seeing the mantle, she changed her mind and decided the piano should definitely go in the living room.

Lottie shook her head as she looked at the windows. This house was everything hers was not: fresh, open, bright and cheery. She staggered when she walked into the kitchen. It was almost the entire width of the house. There was an island in the middle, which Lottie had never seen or heard of before, and more counter space than she knew what she'd do with. The cabinets were beautiful solid oak and the appliances included were a refrigerator, stove with a microwave above, and a dishwasher. She'd never had a dishwasher and microwaves were the latest fad. *I don't know about that contraption, it might give me cancer.* On the far right side of the kitchen was the laundry room. She let out a gasp when she saw a washer and dryer already in place. She grabbed Marie's hand and squeezed it tight. "Lord, I want you to look. A washer and dryer!"

The next room was an office or craft room, as Mrs. Ivey said. It was between the living room and the half bath. It was big enough for a work table and a couple of chairs.

Rebecca raised her hands in the air. "Miss Lottie, this room is perfect for the flower pressing and memory cards. And look, they've already built shelves for your shoe boxes."

All of the excitement was nearly too much for Lottie. She wiped the sweat off her forehead with her handkerchief then fanned herself with the wilted cloth.

"I almost forgot to show you the beautiful screened porch off the kitchen," Mrs. Ivey said.

The porch was three times the size of Lottie's back porch. Ceiling fans hung overhead.

The floor was made of red brick pavers that made an interesting pattern. Lottie stepped outside on the neatly manicured lawn.

"The sellers have been transferred to another state, so of course they couldn't take the storage building with them. There's plenty of room in it and I like where they placed it. The barn style adds charm to the back yard."

The realtor then directed their attention to the lot next door. "Mrs. Johnson, this is such a beautiful piece of land. It's amazing that it's even available. I thought all the lots had been sold when they built these homes five years ago. And you have a garden to transplant here, right?"

"Yes, I have a big garden. It's about an acre and a half. I live on the corner of Kelly and Main."

"Oh, I know where you live. My granddaughter visited your garden on a field trip with the elementary school. She loved your place, said it was so colorful. She even told me about the markers you have out to identify the plants."

"That makes me feel so good to know she enjoyed it. Hopefully she learned some things, too. I'm still planning on having the children visit my garden as long as the school keeps planning the trips."

Rebecca cleared her throat. "Excuse me, Mrs. Ivey, would you mind if we went through the house again?"

"I don't mind at all. Go ahead. Mrs. Johnson, are there any other houses you want to see?"

"No, I really don't. I love this place and with the extra lot, I believe it's meant especially for me and my garden. Don't you think so, Marie?"

"I know it is."

Lottie agreed to show Dovie and Edgar the house if the realtor didn't mind going back. She could show it to everyone in town and not get tired of it. Together they walked down Kelly Street.

"So what's wrong with your car, now?" Lottie asked Dovie.

"I don't know. Ask him."

"I don't know either, not yet, anyway. I still don't see how you could have two hundred fifty-two thousand miles on that car. Where have you been?"

"Listen here, when the Spirit says go, I go. When he says let so-and-so borrow your car, I say yes, Lord."

"Well, you might need to ask the Lord to provide a newer car," Edgar said as he moved behind Lottie. The sidewalk was only wide enough for Dovie and one skinny person; that left him to take up the rear.

"Why don't the three of us pray and ask God for a newer car since we'd all benefit from it." Dovie turned around and winked at Edgar.

"What's going on? What's this us-three-praying stuff?" Lottie asked.

Dovie huffed. "What? You think you got the market on prayer? Can't I pray? Can't Edgar pray?"

"Yeah. But I didn't know prayer was something he did now. I know he used to."

Dovie turned to look at Lottie. "I know God's done miraculous works in you over the past few years, but you still need some maturing in the faith-in-people department."

"You need some help in the watch-where-you're-going department."

"Oh, excuse me, darling," Dovie said after she forced the elderly gentleman flat against the wall of Swift's Dry Cleaner. She shot a quick glance at Lottie. "You could have warned me."

"I guess it's my turn to speak up since I'm part of the three-of-us," Edgar said.

"That's it, Edgar, jump right in there. It don't matter if we in the middle of town. Testify," Dovie said.

He laughed. "Well, I'll try but I'm not going to shout and all that stuff."

"That'll come later with the anointing. Go ahead."

"Lottie, since you don't know any of this, I'll direct my conversation to you. It's been two weeks now—"

Suddenly, Lottie felt a hand shove her in the back, right between the shoulder blades. Her foot stubbed a section of raised sidewalk which sent her body lunging forward. The only thing that stopped her from crashing down, face first on the sidewalk, was a large postal mailbox. It stood on all fours, stout, heavy, and unmovable, as she was thrown into its side. The breath was knocked out of her as blood gushed from a deep cut above her knee.

Lottie heard Dovie scream. The taste of iron filled her mouth before she swallowed the thick, warm liquid. The sound of screeching tires played again in her mind as the pungent odor of burnt rubber stung her nostrils.

When Lottie came to, she was sitting on the sidewalk with her back resting against the cold, rough bricks of Stephens Hardware Store. Someone pressed a cloth to her mouth and commented about stitches needed for the gash on her leg. She reached to rub the back of her head, then she opened her eyes. Edgar, drawn up in a ball, was cradled in Dovie's protective arms. Lottie told him it was okay; everything was all right. But she knew it wasn't. Dovie rocked from side to side as Edgar covered his face and cried. Something was terribly wrong.

Chapter Eighteen

Edgar smoothed the wrinkles from the white blanket after he stood from the bed. He walked to the window and opened the curtains. The street below was busy, filled with traffic and people crossing at the crosswalk. He looked for her among the groups who stepped off the bus; she wasn't there. Then he heard the door open and the sound of Lottie's voice.

"Good, you're awake."

"Yeah. They don't like for you to sleep during the day."

She sat in the chair beside the bed. "Have they brought your lunch yet?"

"No. Soon though."

"Well, what's on the schedule today?"

"Craft time is later. I'll probably finish the painting."

"Tell me, how do you feel, Edgar?" Her eyes were shiny like there was too much liquid in them. The crease between her eyes seemed deeper, more drawn.

He hesitated. "I'm doing better. I saw the doctor earlier and he thinks I'll get to go home in a few days."

"That's good news."

"Well, I can go home if I'm able to do what I need to do."

"What do you mean?"

He sat down on the side of the bed and faced her. "I can't get into that now, but I do need you to do something for me. Are you coming back at seven?"

"I was planning on it."

"Will you bring Dovie with you?"

"Of course I will. Why?"

"I need her to be here for you."

Lottie and Dovie caught the six-thirty bus to Mt. Brayden General, then sat in silence beside each other while life continued in the seats around them. Dovie turned her topaz ring around and around on her finger while Lottie's right leg moved rapidly up and down, causing the seat to shake.

Finally, Dovie spoke. "You don't have no idea why he wants us to come?"

"I told you that three times already. Believe me, if I knew or even had a hint of what he wanted to talk to us about, I'd tell you."

Dovie folded her arms across the huge black pocketbook in her lap. "Let's pray again."

"Right here?"

"God don't ride buses?"

"I mean it's too noisy to pray together. Let's pray silently."

Dr. Preston arrived at Edgar's room just after Lottie and Dovie. Together, they all walked down the hall to a small room with a table and four chairs. After the introductions were made, the doctor proceeded. "We are satisfied with Edgar's improvement and willingness to participate in this last step of his recovery process. The tragic circumstances surrounding the death of Edgar's father and his two cousins, which I understand, Mrs. Johnson, were your husband and daughter, have been hidden from the world and possibly from himself—since Edgar was only a child of eight at the time." He turned and looked at Edgar. "Now, I want you to take as long as you need. Tell them everything that happened the day of the accident."

Edgar's anxiety mounted until the release came through a surge of tears.

"Take your time," Dr. Preston said. "Whenever you're ready."

Edgar cleared his throat. "Since I was eight years old and Jerome, Wy, Daddy, and the driver of the car died, I've blamed myself."

Lottie took a tissue from the box, followed by Dovie.

"That Saturday, I was playing with my basketball in front of the house. I decided to dribble it in the road because it bounced better, even though I was told not to because of the blind curve. Then I saw Jerome walking on the side of the road, coming toward our house. He was on my left. Wy was on his shoulders. He got closer and closer.

"I kept dribbling because I wanted him to see how good I was. I must have dribbled into the far lane because Jerome hollered at me. I don't know what he said, but I remember his voice sounded mad. He took Wy off his shoulders and held her in his arms. Then he started running toward me. I thought I was in trouble. That's when the car came around the curve. I was in the pathway of the car, but Jerome got to me just in time to push me out of the way." Edgar took several deep breaths as his open hand pressed against his chest. "The car swerved to miss me and hit them both. The driver ran into a tree across the road from where I was. He died, but not because he tried to miss Jerome and Wy. He swerved to miss me.

"I had some scratches on my palms where I landed on the side of the road; that was all. I stood up and ran over to where Jerome lay and I saw blood. Wy wasn't close by, she was thrown into a grassy area. I was afraid to look at her up close. Then, I was afraid I'd get in bad trouble, being in the road and all. So I ran to the back of the house and into the barn. I grabbed Daddy's hammer and nails and started hammering nails into a board.

"It wasn't long before I heard the back door slam and Mama calling my name. She ran to me when I stepped out of the barn. She squatted down beside me and hugged me tight. I could hear her heart beating hard and loud against my ear. She said she had heard the crash and was afraid I'd been in the road."

Edgar covered his face with the tissue and wept.

Lottie and Dovie cried softly.

After a few minutes, Edgar continued. "Daddy came running out of the house after Mama. I told them I'd been in the barn building something. Then Mama said let's go see if anybody's hurt and she grabbed my hand, but I wouldn't go. So she and Daddy went."

No one spoke.

"I was the only person who knew what really happened but I couldn't tell anybody. At first, it was because I was afraid I'd get in trouble, but as the years passed, I just couldn't talk about it. It hurt too much. Whenever I thought of it, I'd relive what happened and then Daddy taking his own life a few months later."

Edgar watched Lottie walk to the corner of the tiny room. The muscles around her mouth, cheeks, and chin quivered. Her forehead creased deep. She pressed a handful of tissues to her mouth to quiet herself. It was 1943 all over again.

I don't want to write at all today. For some reason I feel so down. Why, Lord? Looking outside my window I see the primrose and the buttercups growing in the bright sun, but it's not bright inside of me. These old walls have feet, seems like. They step forward and close in around me. I wish Rebecca was here. I guess I got no other choice but to go outside. I'll stand in the sunshine and soak in the light. Why so downcast, oh my soul? If King David could get down at times, is it any wonder I can, too? Mama said I must fight that old devil of depression when he comes sneaking around. I used to laugh at Mama. She was always calling something a devil. She'd say, what you can't see is more real than what you can see, Lottie. Over time I've learned she was right; she was right about everything. As old as I am, I still wish I could lay this weary head in her lap. She'd rub my forehead and tell me, can't no devil in hell mess with you child, unless you let him. You been bought with the precious blood of Jesus and don't you ever forget it.

I tell Rebecca the same thing now. I even rub her forehead like Mama did mine. Why do I still long for Mama? Even as old as I am? I guess no matter how many years pass, you're still somebody's child. After she died I was sitting on the couch, tears flowing. They wouldn't stop. I understood, for the first time, what being an orphan meant. There would never be anyone who would love me like my mama and daddy; no one to remember my birthday or bake me a cake; no one to look at me from across the room and ask, what's wrong, honey? They knew me. I was known and loved. Then they were gone.

Chapter Nineteen

Lottie spotted him coming toward them. Edgar's step was light and his smile, soft and relaxed.

Dovie was the first to throw her arms around him and kiss his cheek. "Come on, Lottie, group hug."

The three of them embraced until the heat forced them apart. On the way to Kelly Street they talked about the hot weather, Dovie's broken-down car which Edgar assured her he would fix right away, and what was for supper later that night.

"Edgar, you should know what we having. It's Friday night," Dovie said.

"Fish?"

"And grits, with hot sauce and tarter sauce, lots of butter on the grits and extra sweet tea with fresh lemon. I made you a peanut butter pie, too."

Lottie chuckled. "That sounds better today than it did at ten o'clock last night. I guess I'll join you after all."

Dovie waved her hand in the air. "Good. You can wash the dishes. This long walk's done ruined my arthritic back."

She not only cleaned up the kitchen after supper that night, but she also swept Dovie's kitchen floor. Lottie was stalling, of course, but she continued to find little things to do like fill the salt and pepper shakers and wipe down the refrigerator shelves. She turned the light on over the stove, closed the curtains, then walked to the living room. "Sorry it took me so long. Dovie's kitchen was a pig sty."

"Well, I can't help it if my girth restricts my cleaning abilities." Dovie pointed her finger at Lottie. "One thing I know for sure is my bathroom is spotless. You could eat off the toilet seat."

"No, thank you," Lottie said.

"Yeah, thanks, but no thanks. I'll use a plate," Edgar added.

Lottie continued to fidget around the room until Dovie asked her what was wrong. "I have something to say to Edgar but I feel like both of you should hear it." She looked at him. "Do you mind if Dovie stays?"

"No."

Dovie whipped her head around. "What do you mean, stays? Ya'll in my house. I guess I could go sit in my clean bathroom with the door shut or go sit outside on the steps and get eat up by mosquitoes. Why don't I go sit in the car and listen to the radio."

"Dovie! He said no."

"Well, okay then. I'll stay."

Lottie sat down on the couch beside Edgar while Dovie sat in the recliner.

"Edgar, the truth about what happened to Jerome and Wy hit me harder than anything since their deaths and the deaths of Mama and Daddy. My heart felt like it was going to explode and bleed forever. But, once I got home and talked it over with the Lord, I saw things from a different perspective. Sure, I lost a lot of years with Jerome and Wy, but what you've carried around, especially as a child, is worse than my loss. I know this sounds bad, but how could you *not* drink? Especially without the Lord to carry those burdens for you. A lot of years I carried mine around too, but I don't anymore.

"Anyway, I'm truly sorry for being harsh with you and for judging you. We never know the depth of pain a person carries in their heart."

"That was beautiful, Lottie," Dovie said as she wiped her eyes with her fingers. "You really should think about going into public speaking or something like that. I mean, I'd be so happy if you'd give my eulogy when I pass. You could pull from so many sources; our friendship being as close as it is and all."

"Stop talking, Dovie." Lottie leaned over to Edgar. Their hug was tight and long. And, for the first time since Edgar was a little boy, she kissed him on the forehead.

Dovie jumped up with her finger pointed toward heaven. "See, that's what I'm talking about. The world didn't give it and the world can't take it away. That's pure love, raining down from the Spirit." She threw her head back and laughed. "Thank ya, Sir."

Tulip

Chapter Twenty

Lottie watched Dovie through the living room window, careful to lift only the edge of the curtain. Her orange, yellow, and olive green floral duster hung loosely from her broad shoulders. She opened the door. "What are you doing here?"

"Thanks for telling me you're moving in two days. Were you gonna wait until the last box was toted out before you said something? Does Edgar, your own flesh and blood, even know?" Dovie grabbed the handle and pulled open the screen door.

Lottie stepped aside and let her through. "I was going to mention it last Friday when we were at the bus stop, but I forgot. Who told you I was moving Thursday, anyway?"

"Leander told Althea; Althea told Hattie; Hattie told Odelia. Me and Odelia was getting our hair done at the beauty shop. She told the whole place, loud as you please, with the dryers going and everything. Don't worry, it's old news now. What can I do to help?" She pulled yellow Playtex gloves from an oversized plastic tote. "I brought duct tape, magic markers, sponges, and ammonia."

"Listen, you really don't need to help. I can handle it."

The lick of her tongue across her lips left them glossy. "Are you forgetting our little secret: pretty cards, flowers on the front, writing on the back? Hmm? I'm not leaving until I help my favorite neighbor pack. Now, if you don't want your secret spread all over town, you'll let me be of service to you."

Lottie shook her head. "That's blackmail."

"Yes, it is. God expects us to help thy neighbor and that's what I'm doing. You helped me that night Aretha gave the best performance of her life. I'm just returning the favor. Now listen, I got tons of moving experience. The most important thing is to move all your kitchen stuff first and get that set up in your new place. Then you'll be able to cook right away. Speaking of cooking, have you fell off, Lottie? You look so frail; ever since the accident. You could stand to put on at least forty or fifty pounds."

Lottie considered the source and ignored the comment. "You can start in the kitchen. The boxes are on the back porch. So are the newspapers. Don't put too much in a box or it'll be too heavy for me to pick up."

"Don't tell me you plan on moving all this stuff yourself. What's wrong with you? I could tote your piano to my house and back, but you? You're a sapling. Skin stretched over bones."

"I've ordered a moving truck and I've paid for two men to come help. Plus, Edgar's taking the day off."

"You sure you're moving Thursday and not Friday? I'd hate to miss out on helping you."

"Go down to the beauty shop and find out."

"Now, now. Don't be like that. Somebody's got to keep up with your business."

Lottie studied Dovie as she talked. Her neck, collared in rolls, was the color of caramel. Large breasts hung underneath her duster like massive bundles of tobacco, suspended from a tall tobacco barn. Her legs were stout but proportionate and her size twelve feet were hard to ignore.

"Dovie, you're so irritating you're likeable."

"Thank you. It's about time you noticed my good qualities. I'll pack up the kitchen. You go on with whatever you was doing before I came. When you get hungry, I got some homemade chicken salad and crackers. I even brought my own tea. Yours ain't quite sweet enough, and I'd just as soon drink water if a glass of tea don't have enough sugar in it." Dovie picked up the bulging fuchsia tote and plopped it on the kitchen table. After digging out the chicken salad and tea, she walked over to the refrigerator and opened the door. "Lord, no wonder you thin as a tithe envelope! You ain't got a lick of food in this fridge!"

Lottie shouted from her bedroom, "Dovie, I'm buying groceries Friday or Saturday. That way I'll have less to move to the new house." Lottie forced herself to remain Christ-like. She reviewed Dovie's good qualities while she cleaned out her nightstand drawer. "Dovie is generous and helpful. She'd give a stranger the clothes off her back, even if the stranger said no. She's a fantastic cook. Dovie makes good chicken salad. She makes very sweet tea. Help me, Jesus, I'm really trying here. Dovie dances good. She's strong, healthy, and able to defend herself against multiple intruders. She really could move my piano to her house. She always smells good. She keeps lipstick on her lips at all times. She's patient. When she calls me, she never hangs up until I answer the phone. I have counted forty-three rings before. That particular day I was not like you, Lord, and I am reminded of your forgiveness. She has nice teeth. Dovie—"

"And now that you're moving so far away, the truth comes out!" Huge tears bubbled over Dovie's round cheeks.

I know you didn't just set me up, Jesus.

Dovie reached down and picked Lottie up off the floor and squeezed her tight. Even though Lottie was five inches taller, her feet dangled high above the floor.

"Dovie Williams, put me down right this minute. I don't know what you think you heard but I was quoting scripture. Let's see. I was talking about the Holy Ghost descending on Jesus like a dove. And when we feed and clothe people, we're acting like Jesus. I talked about patience. Dovie, I said put me down, you gorilla!"

"Well, you don't have to get all nasty about it." Dovie dropped Lottie to her feet. "One minute you giving me the credit I deserve, then the next you disrespecting me. Do you want me to help you pack up or not?" She patted her damp cheeks with a paper towel, tilted her head back at an angle, and stared at Lottie through half-closed eyes. Her right foot tapped. "I'm waiting. You know I've done come up in here to help you pack, trying to be a good neighbor and here you want to go getting all lunaticish on me; acting like you got amnesia or something. Acting like I can't hear good. I know what I heard. Uh huh. You sorry you moving, ain't you? You hate to lose me as a neighbor. I know. I feel the same way. But you ain't moving so far away that ol' Dovie can't come visit. You can have pj parties and I'll spend the night. It's gonna be okay."

Lottie stumbled backward and sat down on the edge of the bed.

"Let me go fix you a plate of my chicken salad and crackers. Now that I know how much you love it, I'll add extra. And my tea, too. No, you can't never have too much sugar in your tea. That's what my mama used to tell me. After you eat, you can take a rest if you need to. I'll finish the kitchen. Don't worry, Lottie, Dovie's here."

After Lottie ate the lunch Dovie made for her, she did rest awhile. What else could she do? Her nerves were so frayed even her feet twitched. Lottie would be lying if she said she never got aggravated with God. She understood that God had an unusual sense of humor, and at times she even appreciated it but not when it was her he was laughing at.

After an hour she got up. Lottie was eager to finish packing the remainder of her bedroom. She walked into the kitchen and found Dovie sitting at the table eating the last of the chicken salad.

"Sleep good? I hope you don't mind but I had to stop packing. I've popped off three of my artificial nails and my lower back is throbbing. I did manage to pack up everything in three of your top cabinets though. Did you know you have two Tupperware gelatin molds?"

"No. You can have one."

"Thank you. I took the oldest-looking one already and put it in my tote bag. I knew you couldn't use two Jell-O molds. Who could? Well, Althea has two. She makes them ambrosia salads for the church socials all the time. She makes herself one and one for the church. She says it's because Lucian complains that she cooks better for the church than she does for him."

Lottie looked at her wristwatch. "Dovie, you've done so much for me already. Why don't you go home now. Especially since your nails have popped off and your back's hurting."

"I'm only gonna say yes if you're sure you can handle the packing by yourself. You know I could always watch TV while you're working in the back rooms. All you'd have to do is holler if you need me."

"I appreciate it, but you know I've been by myself now for a good many years. Even though you're older than me,

I'm still a grown woman. Now, if I get into something I can't handle I know your phone number and I'll call you right over."

"What's my phone number, Lottie Johnson? You don't a bit more know my phone number than you know Clint Eastwood's. Just for that, I'll call *you* later. If I have to be the bigger person and check on you, then so be it. I ain't got no problem with that. Let me get my stuff together and get on over to the house. My grans are probably wondering where I been all day."

"Dovie, you've only been here an hour and a half."

"Still, they'll be worried sick. I can't go nowhere without them tracking me down. They love to talk on the phone, you know. Did I ever tell you about the time we was on the party line and Leander heard us talking about the hat she wore to church? It was pretty, I have to admit, but them little artificial birds had to go." Dovie covered her mouth as she laughed. "Then she comes in church the next Sunday talking all loud, saying, uh huh, some people like to get on that dirty party line and talk about ever body and they brother. Lord have mercy. Leander didn't stop to think she was camping out on that dirty party line, too."

Lottie took Dovie by the arm and steered her toward the door. "Thank you for your help, Dovie. I don't know how you do everything you do."

Dovie smiled big and shrugged. "That's just who I am. It's in my blood."

Thursday morning, Lottie stayed in bed longer than she planned. Her eyes retraced each crack and uneven section of the yellowed plaster wall. She closed her eyes to brand the image in her mind. *How many times have my hands turned the glass knob on the closet door? Does the light fixture hanging overhead know this is the last morning it will look down and smile on me? Will the worn floral linoleum miss the feel of my bare feet in the summer or remember each Lysol bath given after being swept clean?*

Life is not in a house or in things; life is in the living. Stretched out before me is a new chapter in my life. Before, my living was in this space, this setting. But today, I'll walk through wide open doors into a new place. I'll still hear birds singing outside my open window in the morning and smell the flowers as their scent visits my room. They have a new address, like me. I'm not moving alone. Yes, I'll remember this house forever but I won't be sad.

At eight o'clock sharp Lottie opened the front door and looked outside. Instead of Marie and Rebecca, she found Dovie clambering up the front steps, her arms carrying a mound of dishes covered in aluminum foil.

"Hello, Sunshine! It's moving day!"

"I told you I have enough help. What have you got?"

"What does it look like? Me and Leander put together some food for y'all today. It's hard to function on an empty stomach. Odelia pitched in some sausage biscuits. I hope you planned on getting started early. If you want to cook us supper in your new kitchen tonight, you'd better get busy."

"Thank you, Dovie. I take back all the bad things I said about you to Clovis on the phone."

"Like you been on the phone." Dovie chuckled as she cleared a path through the boxes in the living room.

It's going to be a long day.

Seeing Marie, Rebecca and Edgar standing at the front door eased her anxiety. "Come on in," Lottie said.

"Yea, ya'll come on in." Dovie smoothed her hands over her apron. "This is such an exciting day. Even though Lottie's brokenhearted about moving, I think the change will do her good."

Lottie pointed her finger at Dovie. "Don't start with your foolishness. The only thing I'm brokenhearted about is you knowing my new address." *My phone number will be changed.*

Edgar stepped around Marie to answer the knock at the door. Two slender men stood side by side, slightly visible through the screen.

Dovie welcomed them like the owner of the house. "This way. We won't bite. How about a sausage biscuit before y'all get started?"

With that invitation, the two men from We Move it for You walked past Marie and into the kitchen while Lottie and Edgar discussed moving the piano.

In fifteen minutes, Dovie knew more about the two men than she needed to. With her arm raised and finger pointing toward the ceiling, Dovie marched through the living room. "Edgar, Lottie, Marie and Rebecca, into the bedroom." They followed each other in a line. Once inside, Dovie closed the door. "I thought since we gonna be working side-by-side with the movers, I should do a background check."

"Why? They're moving me, not marrying me!" Lottie slapped the side of her thigh.

"Just listen. Ted's the white guy. Even though his hair is long and he doesn't shave, he seems to be okay. He has diabetes. His girlfriend is twenty-two years old and her name is Ramona. They enjoy mountain climbing, horseback riding, and camping. When they get married next summer—"

"Don't tell me. They're going to climb a mountain, pitch a tent, and live on love." Lottie's frustration was building.

Dovie pursed her lips and sighed. "Close. When they get married they're going to start their family of four children and name them after the natural elements. They're naming them—boy or girl—in this order: River, Breeze, Starshine, and Light."

Rebecca held up the peace sign. "Groovy!"

Edgar couldn't listen any longer. "I think I'd better go to the kitchen and keep an eye on things."

Dovie continued. "Darnell Jones, the handsome, well-built black man with a little hair loss, didn't open up as easily as Ted, but I kept prodding."

"You? Prod? That's hard to believe," Lottie smirked.

"Anyway, he's recently divorced but hopes to be reconciled with his ex-wife. He has three children and faithfully pays child support—"

"That's what they all say. Now, honestly, Dovie—"

"His favorite foods are polk salad with scrambled eggs, and chicken: fried, baked, barbequed, grilled, and smoked."

"I got to get out of here. You got too much imagination and too much time on your hands. I'll show your pals what to load first," Lottie said as she walked out of the bedroom.

"I need one last walk through." Lottie straightened her shoulders and lifted her head. She walked through each room without hurrying. Her hand touched each doorknob and light switch tenderly. She felt the bathroom sink's cold porcelain surface while she looked into the frameless mirror hanging in front of her.

She had loved only two men in her life. They had both shaved at this sink; had seen their reflections in this same mirror. Wyonnia splashed here in bubbles. Lottie turned on the cold water, placed her hands underneath, and watched the water wash over her skin. When she was finished she took out her handkerchief and dried her face and hands. She closed her eyes, inhaled slowly, and looked again in the mirror. She closed the door and sat on the edge of the bathtub. Today was bigger than she was.

Dovie sat on the porch swing while Marie and Rebecca sat on the cement steps. Unable to stay quiet any longer, she spoke up. "If I was Lottie I'd take the doorknobs and some of the light fixtures with me. Ain't no rule against mixing the old with the new. If people can put a claw foot tub in their new bathroom, why can't Lottie have some doorknobs and light fixtures changed out?"

Rebecca and Marie looked at each other and smiled.

"Dovie, you're a genius," Marie said.

"That's what I been trying to get across to people. You don't live to be my age without gaining some wisdom. You can't get around it. Every day when I wake up thoughts are swarming around in my head like bees in a beehive. It's shocking. Really. I could be a millionaire if I had someone to back my inventions. Althea and Leander laugh at me but that's all right." She touched her index finger to the side of her head. "It's all up here. Beehive."

Lottie's new home was filled with boxes, bags, furniture, and people. Marie and Dovie unpacked the kitchen items while Rebecca wiped down the bathroom fixtures.

Lottie pulled Edgar into the small craft room. "I meant to ask you earlier but it's been so crazy. Dovie's foolishness just about pushed me over the cliff."

"I know. I was hoping you wouldn't get too rattled."

"I keep humming to myself. Anyway, here's my question. What do you think about moving in the house with me? I've got two extra bedrooms. Rebecca will come over sometimes, but now that she's older, those overnight visits will be less and less."

His eyes, soft and warm, reflected his appreciation and newly deepened love for her. He rested his hands on her shoulders. "As much as I'd love to Lottie, I think I'll stay on with Dovie. She'd be upset if I moved out."

"You two get along that good?"

"I have to admit she's become my second mother. And I try to help around the house when something breaks down or whatever. She depends on me." He smiled. "You don't need me like that; but I'll be over. I'll even spend the night sometimes."

"That sounds like a good deal. But if you ever change your mind or Dovie gets to be too much to handle, just let me know. My home is open to you."

"Thank you. Just to know that means the world to me."

Ted and Darnell installed the light fixtures and door knobs from the old house which added charm and familiarity. Lottie felt at home instantly. They also placed a concrete fountain in the center of the vacant lot beside the house. Three smiling cherubs effortlessly balanced three sections of bowls, each high above the other. Lottie sat in a green lounge chair and listened as the water cascaded over the smaller bowls and splashed into the larger one.

The vacant lot transform into a landscape filled with familiar faces. Her Don Juan rose bush looked strong and determined as Mr. Gossett, the landscaper, lowered him into his new home. He would be enjoyed from her bedroom window upstairs as well as from her living room windows which faced the garden. Her hydrangeas: Annabelle, Nikko Blue, Penny Mac, and Endless Summer, remained hearty even after the bumpy ride over. Lottie chose their partially-shaded spot close to the back of the lot in hopes that they would feel free to stretch and grow even bigger. Her hummingbird bush, which never had a problem stretching, was placed in the eastern corner of the lot to continue its free, untamed life. Hostas, daylilies, azaleas, and rose bushes were placed carefully into the welcoming soil.

While Mr. Gossett planted four pink dogwoods in the front of the garden, facing the street, his partner lay a careful footpath made of limestone, quarried from the town of Pacolet, just a few miles away. At the end of two days, all that remained unearthed were neat symmetrical squares, rectangles and half circles. They would be filled with bulbs: tulips, daffodils, crocus, alliums, hyacinths, lilies, and jonquils.

The finishing touch would be a black wrought-iron fence, protective but open and inviting; unlike the fence Jerome built all those years ago. Lottie liked to think of this fence as a frame placed around an ever changing, colorful work of art, free to be enjoyed by all who pass by.

Dovie stopped by today for lunch. I knew she was upset about something. She told me she went to get her license renewed and they turned her down. Her eyesight is getting worse and she's been having spells with her sugar. I should have known that by the way her Buick swayed down the highway back when we went to the peach shed.

She was upset about it and I don't blame her. She used to carry all us around in that old car of hers. One summer Dovie took me, Leander, Althea, and Clovis to the Thunderbird Drive-In over in Spartanburg. We saw

Clint Eastwood in A Fist Full of Dollars and For a Few Dollars More. I never told any of them, but I was in love with Clint Eastwood. He was the best-looking white man I'd ever seen. I guess we all loved him. We never talked through the movies either. Even Dovie was quiet. We all brought food from home: cold chicken, biscuits, fried potatoes. Stuff like that. I told Dovie not to worry about it. That she'd be able to get around on the bus good enough. She agreed, but I could tell she was heartbroken. I realized then that a season in our lives had come to a sad end.

I'll be beholding to Dovie for the rest of my life, but I don't know if I'll ever tell her. It was her idea to bring some of the old light fixtures and door knobs over. They add a special touch. It was my idea to bring over the mirror from the bathroom. It's hanging in Rebecca's room. Dovie wants me to have a party soon; I'm not so sure about that. I don't want to get kicked out of the neighborhood, I just got here.

Fourteen summers later

Chapter Twenty-One

He turned off the water hose by the Don Juan and gently flicked a bug off one of the petals. The iris bulbs, placed in the cold earth years before, now returned, tall and sturdy with thin, velvety extensions like fingers ready to grasp sunlight, dew, and rain. Colorful life surrounded him.

Edgar took off his shoes at the back porch and walked into the kitchen in his socks. He glanced at the clock, then walked to her bedroom door and knocked. "Lottie, it's almost time to go. Are you ready?"

"Come in, Edgar." She sat on the edge of the bed in her robe. Her hair was brushed and fixed and clustered earbobs were clipped to her earlobes, but she wasn't dressed. She stared ahead with her thin hands folded in her lap.

Edgar sat down beside her. "Listen, in about an hour, hundreds of people are going to be sitting at the ball field, waiting to see you."

"I know. I just don't know if I can do it. I'm scared. My stomach is flopping around and I've been to the bathroom so many times I'm dizzy. I wish Ann had just left my memory cards alone."

"Don't say that. And remember, they never were your memory cards."

"You know what I mean. I made them because that's what God told me to do. I always keep my end of a deal. I never intended for them to be put in a book, though. And now I got to go stand in front of all those people and talk; I just don't think I can do it."

"Lottie, I know you better than anybody in the whole world, even better than I know Dovie. If there's a woman who can stand before a large crowd of people and speak from her heart, it's Lottie Johnson. Now, there are too many people depending on you. Dovie said she's getting a good seat up front so she can help you if you mess up."

"Oh, great. That's all I need." She laughed and covered her mouth.

Edgar walked to the closet and opened the door. "Now, what dress do you want?"

"The tan one with the white collar."

He took the dress off the hanger and laid it on the bed. "Now, get moving. You don't want to be late and have to walk in front of all those people do you?" He stepped out of the room.

"I've already got to speak in front of them. What's the difference?" she said loudly. Edgar heard Lottie's footsteps nearing the door. She stepped out of the room. "You look beautiful," he said.

"Thank you. I guess we'd better get this thing over with. I'm telling you now, if I'd ever known Ann was sending my cards to a publisher I'd never have let her keep them at the library. She was suppose to preserve them for me, you know."

"I know. We've been through this a hundred times, now let's go."

She picked the pocketbook up off the counter and walked through the living room. He opened the door of the Cutlass and helped her in. "By the way, I've got to speak today, too. Does that make you feel better?"

"I didn't know that. No, it doesn't make me feel better. Now I have to worry about both of us messing up."

He chuckled as he drove away. The traffic was lined up past Fletcher's all the way down Main and back behind the elementary school. He had to tell one of the officers directing traffic that he was carrying the guest of honor and needed to get through the crowd.

"Well, why didn't you say so? We'll get her in," the officer said.

When they made it to the platform and sat down, Edgar pulled out his handkerchief and wiped his face. His back relaxed. He could see Dovie, right in front of them, waving and smiling. Marie and Ann sat to the left of Dovie. Rebecca and David, more in love now than when they married, sat on either side of Rosie, their seven-year-old daughter.

Edgar leaned in close to Lottie's ear. "Feel better?"

"No. I think I'm going to vomit."

"It'll all be over in less than thirty minutes. You can hang on that long. And Lottie, try to enjoy it. Things like this don't happen everyday. Face it—you're a celebrity." He laughed louder than he intended and immediately saw the disapproval in Lottie's dark eyes.

Cecil Radcliff III stepped in front of Lottie and shook her hand. Ann left her seat, walked up on the platform, and pinned a large corsage of roses below Lottie's collar at the same time a young guy with hair past his shoulders, tested the sound system.

Edgar decided there could not have been a more perfect day. It was May in Mt. Brayden. The sun was warm on the skin, the birds sang soft melodies, and the blooms and blossoms sweetened the air. He snapped out of his daydreaming when he saw the young man hand the microphone to the mayor.

The portly gentleman worked his way behind the podium. It was obvious to Edgar the man was miserable. He perspired from a suit too heavy; walked in shoes too small; and choked from a tie too tight. "Hello, good people of Mt. Brayden. What else can I say except it's a wonderful time to be Mayor." He smiled as he looked over the crowd. "What an honor to be seated on this platform today with such an outstanding example of selflessness. I wish I'd sent my wife more flowers, especially seeing how many wives got them regularly from their husbands." He laughed and turned and looked at Edgar. "I have purposely kept it short because I want Mr. Edgar Dewberry to have the honor of introducing his lovely cousin and our guest of honor, Mrs. Lottie Johnson. Good people of Mt. Brayden, Mr. Edgar Dewberry."

The crowd applauded while Edgar took his paper from his jacket pocket. *Here I am trying to calm her down and look at me. I'm shaking all over.* He straightened his tie and stepped to the podium. The microphone broadcasted his sigh so loud it startled him; his stomach churned. Then he found Dovie again on the front row.

She nodded her head and smiled.

"Good afternoon, ladies and gentlemen. As Mayor Royster said, I am Edgar Dewberry, Lottie Johnson's cousin. On the ride over, Mrs. Johnson asked me to personally thank each of you for this wonderful display of affection and honor. She will speak shortly, but she insisted that you all be thanked first.

"I remember when Lottie showed me her memory cards. At that time, they only filled a few shoe boxes hidden under her bed. I believe forty-two boxes were placed with Ann two years ago. Obviously Lottie believed in the importance of keeping memories alive, sharing with others all the love and thoughtfulness that make up the town of Mr. Brayden.

Flowers were sent for anniversaries, birthdays, weddings, and proms. When someone lost their loved one, flowers were sent; if a family member or friend was hospitalized, flowers were sent. Sometimes they were sent simply to say I love you or I'm thinking of you.

"When Ann Whiteside, our librarian, called me and told me she was editing and submitting the memory cards to a publishing friend of hers at Peacock Press, I thought, well, that's nice, he'll probably enjoy looking at a few, but that's as far as it will go. Now, as you all know, Lottie's book, *Practical Love—A Documented History of Loving Kindness,* has not only been a huge seller but has also put Mt. Brayden, South Carolina, on the map."

Cheers and applause rose from the crowd.

Edgar breathed deep. His pride for Lottie mounted.

"That's the reason we're all here today—to celebrate Lottie Johnson, our town, and our people. Because of the success of *Practical Love,* Mt. Brayden will finally have a recreational park to be proud of and enjoyed for years to come. Not only will the park have picnic areas, but also fountains, because of Lottie's great love for them. And, of course, there will be lots and lots of flowers. Walking trails and plenty of benches under shade trees will encourage people to come out and enjoy the fresh air and sunshine. The park will be named Johnson Park as a memorial to her and her family. And now, I present Mt. Brayden's own, Lottie Johnson." He turned around and faced her as she stood to speak. Edgar smiled and gave her a gentle hug.

Lottie clutched her notes in her hand. She closed her eyes and exhaled slowly. Then she spoke. "Thank you is made up of only two words, but as I say thank you, Mt. Brayden, know that these simple words hold vast amounts of gratitude and love."

"First, in case some of you here believe me to be a saint who wanted to lay down her life for her town—here's the truth: it was out of a heart filled with hurt and anger that memory cards were born. They were God's answer to a bitter woman's prayer; just as simple as that. And you, wonderful people of Mt. Brayden—the Gahagans, Shippys, Kimbrells, Hendersons, and countless others, too many to name—supplied the subject matter just by loving those around you. Did you realize a flower sent for an anniversary, or birthday, or prom, or thank you would impact the world around you? No, and neither did I, as I set out to press each flower and create each card.

"Twenty years ago I was unable to read and write adequately and too proud to do anything about it until love in the purest form—a little girl with a heart that believed I could do anything—shared her homework with me.

"Years ago I was unable to love with unconditional love until a wise and godly woman cared enough for me to speak the truth when I didn't want to hear it.

"Years ago a young man whose childhood, damaged and marred by tragedy, taught me that no matter how great my pain or loss, my heartache or suffering, someone, somewhere endured more—suffered more—and lost more that I could ever imagine.

"You may be asking, 'Lottie, what are you trying to tell us?' I stand before you today with some important words that have the power to change your life. You may forget most of what I've said, but don't miss this: remember love and have faith in God.

"In the Old Testament, Joshua set up stones of remembrance. When their children asked what the stones were for, they were to tell them that twelve stones were gathered to represent the twelve tribes and heaped in a mound as a reminder and memorial of God's rescue through the parting of the Jordan River.

"Today, I encourage you to do what Joshua did. When you don't have money to buy your next meal, remember how God provided before, then remember love and have faith. When the pain of losing someone you love tries to swallow you up, remember that loved one: their eyes, their voice, their smile. Smell their scent; feel their touch. They are as close as your next breath. Remember love and have faith. When you feel like you can't go on and life is not worth living, don't give up. Remember the God who loves you. Remember His son, His sacrifice, His promises. He said I will never leave you nor forsake you. Remember love and have faith in God.

"So even though I stand before you today and receive applause and recognition, understand that I, more than anyone here, remember well each stone of remembrance in my heap, my mound.

"I close with these words, applied like ointment to my heart on one of my darkest days. Who can measure the effects of love and kindness? They are far reaching, unbinding and eternal."

Thunderous applause continued after Lottie sat down beside Edgar. He turned and looked at her face. She stared at something beyond the stage, past the standing crowd, and into the park. She moistened her parted lips. Edgar heard her gasp, and quickly turned to follow her gaze.

And, there they were, walking toward the stage: Jerome, forever young in his gleaming white shirt and black creased pants, kept his eyes fixed on Lottie. Wyonnia, in pink ruffles and checks, smiled and giggled in her daddy's arms.

Edgar rubbed his eyes, then looked at Lottie again. He had never seen that smile before.

Suddenly she glanced at Edgar and then back at Jerome. Lottie lifted her trembling hand and leaned forward. Jerome and Wy, together, held one red Don Juan rose.

The crowd continued to cheer. Edgar wiped his eyes again and waited. Then, in what seemed like slow motion, Lottie's glowing face turned. Edgar looked into her tear-filled eyes.

"You saw them, didn't you?"

Edgar smiled and took her hand. "I saw them."